BODKIN

BODKIN

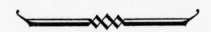

BARTON MIDWOOD

RANDOM HOUSE NEW YORK

Library of Congress Catalog Card Number: 67-14469

Manufactured in the United States of America
by The Haddon Craftsmen, Inc., Scranton, Pennsylvania

Designed by Carl Weiss

CONTENTS

{ BODKIN }

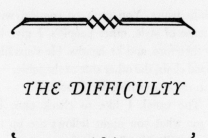

THE DIFFICULTY

The children are asleep. I'm alone in my sitting room with a book. I am one of five night watchmen in this place, a treatment center for disturbed boys. I'm reading—a fragile, aery fiasco replete with palace, beadsman and lovers. A mist drifts over the type. The merest breath, and everything will go to pieces in your hands. You have to turn the pages, even the pages, very carefully. We're well into the night, my book and I; the radiators keep time. There are footsteps on the stairs . . .

It's Pincher, for sure; I know the sound of his shoes. I slip my marker in the leaves. The building, the whole rickety edifice, groans.

"Hello, Bodkin," he says. "Any trouble?"

"Everything's under control. I've locked ten of them in the john."

It gives him pause. You can't be comical with Pincher; he has no sense of style, other people's. I give him a wink and a smile therefore, and he laughs. He slaps his knees and sits in the hard chair, the other side of the table.

"Putting in some overtime, Mr. Pincher?"

"Oh no. The usual. I like to check once in a while, Bodkin, to see what you night fellows are up to. I caught Boober just now. Sleeping."

"Really? That's not like Boob. He's the most conscientious of us all."

"Yes, I know. It's unusual for him. Nevertheless, Bodkin, we've got to stay awake."

"I know."

"At all times. One never can tell when an emergency might arise."

"Very true, Mr. Pincher."

"You fellows are paid to keep your eyes open. We ask nothing more of you. It's the simplest sort of job."

"I know."

"On the other hand, it's difficult. To stay awake all night. I remember when I was an ensign, in the Navy—"

"You were an ensign, were you."

"Ah yes . . ."

He launches into that, the Navy, his adventures. He passes the night like water, like stones. You'd think he'd want to be home in bed, but he'd rather drive me to distraction. He combats boredom by torturing more vigorous minds with his own torpidity. It's a weapon with which he is cavalier. He's a big man. He married a white woman. I've never seen her. They say she's no beauty. Two of them here have married white. Pincher and Port. Why's that? Dissembling the races. Pincher himself is rather a hybrid. He is light-skinned and wears middling suits. He turns up his nose at the peculiar style of his race, Pincher does, and puts on the fashions of the white, the solemn rat race that he loves with a vengeance. But he can't, you see, try as he may, get the drift of our dances—our minuets, our waltzes, our swans. You've got to have the toes for it, a certain kind of an ear. Give Pincher something to parrot, and he'll give you back inevitably the thing's most hideous features. I've written him off, but he nettles me all the same. He has a charm, which is finally his most annoying feature, because it won't let me dismiss him quite as satirically as I ought to. He styles himself the Chancellor. "Keeper of the King's Conscience," he likes to say, in his colorful moments. It serves well enough as a title and saves him the embarrassment of being referred to as the assistant . . . to the director, who is white. I've become race-conscious here, I'm outnumbered. The Lord High Chancellor indeed.

At about four in the morning, just when it's beginning to brighten up outside and I'm vanquished and at sea, having been assaulted for three hours by his entire fleet, his guns, his gales, his whores and his chaplain, "Somebody, Bodkin," he says, "is attempting to kill Director Doberman."

"Yes, I know."

"We've tried to keep it quiet, but that's impossible, of course. Everyone is talking. It's got quite out of hand. The rumors are dangerously imaginative. It's reached even the boys . . . Bodkin, I need your help. No, no, don't say no. This is an emergency. Who else can I turn to? You've been here longer than most of us. I need someone I can trust, to keep an eye on the night watchmen. To make reports—discreetly, you understand—on their behavior."

He goes on about it. It's tedious, that's the principal

thing. I'd finish the old man myself, given the opportunity, just to put an end to the hoopla once and for all. But there'll be no end, ever, to give a fellow satisfaction. Pincher wants to bore me to death, that is his aim in life. The pity is he can't succeed soon enough to suit anyone's taste. One dies of something else altogether. "I'll have nothing to do with the affair," I tell him. "I am an observer of the human condition," not mincing my words, no, playing my highest hand. "It's six of one, half a dozen of the other, so far as I'm concerned. Let them kill him. Let them kill me too. Let them kill everyone. What does it all amount to anyway in the long run, Pincher?"

But no, he won't have it. Observer indeed. In fact, it's a mistake; I've taken the wrong line with him, one on which he can hang up his bones and rattle your brains. One loves quiet after all, above everything, and has to have it. He has banked on that, strategically. He makes one bog of a din. He needs me, Pincher does. To make reports. To watch the watchmen. One relents, that's all there is about it. He shakes my hand gratefully and leaves.

There has never been a tower tall enough to escape the yacking. I've been to the top of the Empire State, had a whiff of the nebulae; you can hear the bleat of the taxicabs, the pedestrians. They even clap a pair of earphones on those fellows who are rocketed out to the nether world; a wise guy, an earthling, gives them the latest views. Now there is a conquest to make one gape. We have to keep each other in tow. There is a certain amount of good sense to it.

My book. I return to my book. It has fallen apart— palace, beadsman and lovers, the very verses themselves, all—shattered into a thousand fragments, irrecoverable.

THE SPY

In cases of this sort, sleep is the best bet. I put my head in my hands on the tabletop and summon the gargoyles, the imps, the fears, the tremblings, the most prodigious amusements in my little bag of tricks. But then, just when things are beginning to shape up, Boober's voice breaks in and he claps me on the shoulder.

"Do not fear, my friend, that I suppose you to have been asleep just now," he says. "Likely you find that an excellent position in which to meditate."

"What time is it?"

"It is dawn, my friend. It is dawn. It is that time when

yesterday's lack of fulfillment rises up cheerfully, to welcome with open arms the new day's hideous lack of promise. If ever I go mad, Bodkin, it will be at dawn. In the meantime, one must accept one's fate, one must not attempt to run away from suffering. In suffering lies beauty, my friend, and the very meaning of life itself. This is what I have learned tonight."

"That's what you've learned every night I've known you, Boober."

"Indeed it is a lesson I have rehearsed over and over. And over again. It never ceases to amaze me. It is five o'clock." He puts his watch back in his waistcoat, eases himself into a chair and smiles sweetly at me.

Boober is a very large man and is occasionally addressed as "Fatso" by certain persons. Trembley and Ashe, the watchmen from the other wing, drift in. I hadn't heard them in the passage. That's it then, the night shot to hell. They want to talk. They nod at me and take seats, one on either side of Boober. They're always following him about, these two. They even tag along after him on weekends, on his nights off. Trembley and Ashe met originally in a freight car and have despised each other ever since. Boober contains their friendship for them, provides them with a train of thought. They're transported by his relentless jabber and let it take them where it will.

"Pincher was up to see me tonight," I say. "About Doberman. The murder attempts."

Boober has a lot of tears in his eyes tonight. He makes no answer.

"I just thought I'd let you know," I say, "that Pincher's asked me to spy on you guys—"

"Eh?"

"To make reports."

"Did he mention my name, Bodkin?"

"Nobody's name. I'm not supposed to be telling anyone this, you understand. I could lose my job."

Boober wrinkles his brow. "Do you mean to say—"

"He's nuts, that's what I mean to say. If I had fifty bucks and a bus ticket, fellas, I'd quit on the spot."

"D'you mean to say, lad, that he suspects *us?*" says Trembley.

"Me?" says Ashe.

"No," says Boober, "I cannot accept it. I shall speak to Pincher directly."

"You've got to keep your mouth shut, Boober. I could lose my job I told you."

"Really? Well then, I shall not say a word. For your sake, Bodkin. Besides, it is beneath my dignity." The tears are streaming down his face.

"What *is* it you're bawling about all the time, Boober?"

He blinks at me, taken aback by this. He glances from Trembley to Ashe and then manages to pull himself together with some pride. "It is a great happiness to me, weeping," he says.

"No kidding."

"Yes. Once I told that to Pincher. He called me an egoist. And then when I laughed, he proceeded to call me a lot of nasty names from a psychology text he'd been reading. He is keen on the subject and eager to impress Dr. Sweeney, who only despises him for it."

"Unfairly, I think," says Ashe, "for Pincher has a firm grasp of the subject."

"That is true, Ashe. He diagnosed me, at any rate, quite perceptively—to no good effect, I might add. He caused me to be ashamed, and I stopped weeping for several weeks.

[9]

The nights were joyless during that period; I had nothing any more. As soon as I realized this, I took up my weeping again. Why not? I said to myself."

"Certainly there are baser entertainments," says Ashe, with a stern look at Trembley, who is nipping at his grog.

Boober looks at me imploringly. "And I hurt no one by it. What do you think, Bodkin? Do I hurt anyone by it? Please tell me. At once! For if I hurt anyone in any way whatsoever by my weeping, I shall stop."

"Of course not," I say. "But it is, frankly, Boober, something of a pain in the neck. Not to myself, naturally, because you're my friend. But to other people. They don't like it. You ought to take up something a bit more serious. Then you wouldn't have people worrying about your marbles all the time. Like me, see? I read. When Pincher comes up he finds me at a book, and he says to himself: Ah, that Bodkin, he's always improving his mind—a fine fellow! And he doesn't bother his head about me any further. But you, Boober, he doesn't quite know what to make of you, a grown man crying his eyes out all night. He's confused. Now he even suspects you of attempted murder; that's where your weeping's got you. You've got to try and change yourself a little, Boob, if you expect to get along in this world. Really, you may not always be so lucky. The next fellow who spies on you probably won't have your best interests at heart. He may think up something extraordinary to titillate the big shots with, just so he can get ahead a little himself. Why don't you take up basket-weaving or something?"

"But I am so clumsy." Boober sighs. "Each time I have attempted to be useful, I have been the reverse."

"People swear at him," says Trembley.

"Yesterday," says Boober, "I attempted to help an elderly woman cross an intersection. I carried her bundle for her and dropped it. It contained glassware. She sat on the curb and wept. I sat down and wept with her. I put my arm around her to console her. She gave a start and said nasty psychological things to me. She accused me also of having designs on her virginity. So I left. I did not know she was a virgin. Although had I known, I should have certainly had designs. Not out of lust, for she was no longer provocative, the poor dear, but out of pity. It is pitiful for a woman to die a virgin."

"Boober has always been specially concerned about nuns, in fact," says Ashe.

"But alas, there too one's hands are tied. No, with women I have never been successful. As soon as I begin to demonstrate my passions, I am taken for a beast. I am overly enthusiastic. I frighten women. Weeping . . . weeping is my only pleasure now. It comes easily to me. Laughter comes hard. I have been educated badly. If I could laugh more easily, I would take up laughing. But then, you see, inappropriate laughter—it too makes people suspicious— even more than inappropriate weeping does—because weeping, I suppose, is somehow never quite . . . entirely inappropriate. If you follow my drift."

He hasn't heard a thing I've said to him.

"The principal idea I'm trying to get across to you, Boober, is you've got to find something to occupy yourself with—d'you know? To keep up appearances. Something that's not so out and out melancholy. Reading, for example —that's easy enough. You don't even have actually to read anything. Just hold a book in your hands and keep it right side up. It'd solve your whole problem. Who knows, you might even get interested in it after a while. I've got some books I can let you have, if you like. Lots of racy ones too, with pictures."

"Reading?" Boober says, and he blows his nose. "Ah, reading. Well yes, that is certainly something to ponder. And I am profoundly moved, believe me, by your generous offer. I did some reading once, but of course a very modest amount, and not very systematically."

"What's the last book you read, Boober?" I say.

He blushes and glances at Trembley, who is staring into his bourbon, and then at Ashe, who is mumbling to himself. Then he turns, slowly, his big sad eyes on me, and lets them rest there.

"I can tell you the book," he says. "Does this surprise you, Bodkin? There were two books, in fact. I was reading them simultaneously—the verses of Saint John of the Cross, and an excellent little English grammar . . . participles, infinitives, gerunds—wonderful creatures. They haunt me still. 'Boober,' they seem to say to me, 'you are good, after all. Though on the surface what you say seems foolish and base, at bottom runs a stern logic. And logic is good. At bottom, then, you are good. We have studied and we know. You are good. You are logical.' It makes me weep— do you know? So you can see, Bodkin, that for a man who weeps even over a grammar, reading is not the solution either."

"What about Saint John of the Cross? Did you weep over that too?"

"Well, he was not so moving as the grammar, Bodkin, but he is exquisite all the same— What's that?"

It's footsteps, somebody stalking about somewhere. That's Weasel, for sure.

"That," says Boober, "would be Weasel." He jumps up from his chair, puts his ear against the wall and rolls his eyes up at the ceiling. "Why does he persist?" he says. "He has been here nearly as long as I have, and yet—" He looks at me. "How long have I been here, Bodkin?"

"Eight years."

"A long time!" he cries, and then he lowers his voice to a piercing malicious whisper: "Yet he persists. And do you know why?"

"Because he is *unchristian*," says Ashe, emulating Boober's whisper.

Ashe is quite angry and excited about it. Both he and Boober are angry and excited, I guess. They start to breathe heavily; their eyes are full of fire, and they're red in the face. Weasel brings out the best in them.

"That Weasel!" cries Boober, and he begins to wave his arms about wildly, to pace up and down the room, the floorboards groaning under him. " 'I am conscientious, Boober,' he is fond of telling me. Conscientious! Did you ever? Weasel investigates his thirty-six beds every half-hour, twenty-two times, every single night! Can you imagine? Multiply that by eight years, Bodkin, and you will arrive at an appalling product. But I ask you, what has he accomplished with his conscientiousness? As soon as one of the children so much as blinks at the flashlight, Weasel has him by the scruff of the neck—one, two!—and into his sitting room. Tonight there are five of his weary urchins in pajamas, standing at attention around his desk. He will keep them there until the day shift arrives. This—do you see?—this is what he has accomplished! Did you know that he sometimes pokes them with a needle to keep them awake?"

"He's not so bad as you make him out," I say.

"This *too* is possible," Boober says. He picks up my book absently and shakes it at me as he talks. The marker falls out; he's lost my place. He says, "But you, Bodkin, you and I are of the same temper. Tell me, when was it you last made the rounds?"

"I don't remember."

"And have you had any trouble? No. Do you see? It is only Weasel who has trouble. Because he is conscientious. But you had trouble at first, did you not, when you were conscientious? I remember the stories you told me. 'Boober,' you said when I first arrived, 'sit still. Let the night take care of itself.' Had I listened, I should have been spared a year's anguish. One must learn one's own lessons. But Weasel will never learn. And now they suspect us of having designs on Doberman's life. Well, and what do you make of that? Weasel, I suppose, is to be exempt from suspicion."

"No, he's not exempt."

"I should say not! He is the only watchman conscientious enough to be capable of such an absurdity! The rest of us are preoccupied. Trembley tipples, Ashe prays, you read and I, Casey Boober . . . weep! That leaves Weasel. He has no hobby. He is your man. And yet, at bottom, he is a good soul and lacks the courage. Clearly, it's a mistake."

"And beyond that," says Ashe, "an insult."

"A rotten trick," says Trembley.

"Why didn't Pincher confront *us* with this obscenity of his?" cries Boober. "Eight years, Bodkin! I cannot bear this everlasting secrecy. This lack of trust. I cannot tolerate spies."

He can't tolerate spies. All right, good enough. And he

looks at me quite hatefully. What's that mean? Spit and
tears all over his coat. It's revolting. One ought to keep
one's mouth shut, an old maxim I keep forgetting. I want a
little peace and quiet. I want my palace, my lovers. It's not
so easy. They'll sit here all night if I let them. I'd throw
them out, but I haven't the inclination. I'll go out for a
breath of air and leave them alone in my quarters; they'll
get the message after a bit. I pick up my marker, take my
little book gently out of his hands and go to the door.

"See you fellows at breakfast."

PREMONITIONS

I head across the courtyard. Maybe I can read out here. A light fresh snow is falling. Miss Rose, the nurse, comes out of Weasel's quarters. She's trying to run, it seems; her head is tucked way down into her collar. She has only a thin coat on over her flannel gown, and her feet are bare save for a pair of thin slippers flapping at the heels. She's clutching the top of the coat to her throat with one hand; she hasn't bothered to button it. She's old, old, and spry, built like a Christmas tree. Her hair, black mainly, is wrapped in a bun at the nape. I saw her once with it down; it is old and dry and hangs to her knees. She has an apartment on the premises, the only one on the staff who does.

It's next to the infirmary. The fevers there keep her in a sweat of a night. She is a Jew, and not well liked. The smaller boys take to her some at first, but they age soon enough. It's a thankless task, but she has nowhere else to go. She is a Canadian, with a dash of British in her blab, and bears a lofty disdain for the mysteries of her race. She says she knows nothing about it, but the features tell. Rosie, Rosie, Jewie Nosie. I've seen photographs of her in her bloom. Ugly and Semitic as sin, she would have been a wallflower even in Jerusalem. A face is a lamentable, terrible thing.

I catch up to her just as she is about to enter the building. She whirls around and glares. I'm the voice in an empty yard.

"You frightened me half to death, young man."

"I'm sorry."

"Sorry! A lot of good's in sorry!" She squints at me. "Who is it, anyway? I haven't my specs."

"It's me. Bodkin."

"Of course. Bodkin. I knew your voice. Well? Come in, come in. You'll catch your death."

We go into the dirty little vestibule adjacent to the treasurer's office. Her apartment is just up the staircase.

"Any trouble?" I say.

"It's nothing, nothing. I'm becoming intuitive. It's a disgrace."

"Where have you been just now?"

"To Weasel's quarters. Group Five."

"Is somebody sick there?"

"No. Here." She points to her head. "Ah God! What's to become of me?"

"There, there." I touch her shoulder.

She gives a start. "Don't touch me, young man. What do you think? Eh? I'm quite . . . quite capable!"

"I'm sorry—"

"Sorry! A lot of good's in sorry! Listen to me. Do you know where I've been?"

"Group Five. Weasel's quarters."

"Who told you that?" Her eyes bulge; she's amazed. "Word's got about already—God! Or perhaps you're spying on me . . . is that it? Well? Speak up!"

"You told me yourself, Miss Rose, just a moment ago that you'd been to Group Five."

"Did I? Truly?"

I nod and smile at her as reassuringly as I can. I'm not much good at it though.

"It's coming to that too, is it?" she says. "The memory going as well, along with everything else. Just sneaking out of my head!"

"You're just overwrought. Everybody forgets. I forget things all the time, and I'm young."

"And an idiot as well . . . a sorry consolation. I am a woman of science, sir. Can you comprehend that? I have chipped and honed this old brain of mine into an acute instrument. Too sharp, I'm afraid, too fine—it won't hold together. It's crumbling away, like so many grains of sand."

I take her elbow gently. I'll lead her up the stairs to her apartment. I don't know what to do. What should I do?

"Now, now," I say. "Get a grip, Miss Rose. You're over-doing it a bit. They'll be coming for sick call in another hour. The boys depend on you. It's just an unsettling time of day. Dawn's hard. Nothing seems right with us. Tell me about your science, why don't you? Are you doing research or something? It is a pleasant surprise, really, to discover that your interest in scientific matters goes so far beyond that of the ordinary nurse. Why don't we go up and have some tea?"

"Tea indeed!" she cries, and pulls away from me. "In my apartment? Tea? Do you realize to whom you are speaking? Take your hands off me. I am not an invalid!"

When I let her loose she goes to pieces, buries her face in her hands and sobs and gasps.

The infirmary door at the head of the stairs opens. Bunsen, one of the new arrivals, a sickly eight-year-old, appears, a dark foreign continent spread over the front of his pajamas.

Miss Rose snaps out at him. "Back to bed, child."

He disappears and she falls into my chest, as I'm the closest thing to hand, and has it out in there.

"Here. Have my handkerchief. It's clean."

"Thanks." She blows her nose fiercely, dries her eyes and then sits down on the foot of the staircase, quite worn out.

By and by she pulls herself together. "Forgive me, Bodkin. I'm so . . . I had a premonition, you see. Some little fellow is deathly ill in Group Five, I said to myself. I sat up in bed. I went over to Weasel's. I felt foreheads, I took pulses—healthy as horses, all of them. I'm an old woman. I have premonitions, the mind's not what it used to be. I'm overwrought, Bodkin, overworked. I didn't mean a word of what I said to you."

"What did Weasel say?"

"He was reserved. He is a nice quiet man, conscientious. I suppose he'll be talking though. Miss Rose is slipping, he'll be saying. But perhaps he won't. He *is* quiet, and kind as well. Isn't he? Yes, I think so."

"What was he doing though, when you came in?"

She narrows her eyes, and looks at me oddly. "Doing?" she says. "He was keeping five boys company in his sitting room."

"You don't say. What for, I wonder. Did you ask?"

"Of course. And he turned the most sympathetic eye upon me and said, 'Miss Rose, they're having a little trouble getting to sleep tonight. I'm entertaining them.' And then he winked at me, in that sympathetic gentlemanly way he has. He is reallly quite dedicated, with a great affection for the boys. Imagine! Entertaining them at that hour of the morning."

"And what did the boys say?"

She is put out that I'm pressing her, but it's delicate and she manages to keep up her end. "The boys?" she says with a touch of amazement. "They never said a word. They're well behaved with Weasel. They don't interrupt him. They re*spect* him, Bodkin." This is intended as an insult to me, but I simply smile, and she tries to change the subject. "You know, I don't think he'll be talking about me. He's not one given to gossip. What do you think?"

Somebody is shuffling about in the treasurer's office. I look at the door—the rustle of papers, the safe creaking on its hinges—and smile at Miss Rose. She glances nervously at the door too and starts in a panic up the stairs. I hold her back.

"Let go of me, young man!"

"Sometime I'd like to have a talk with you, Miss Rose."

"About what?" She is beside herself.

"Things."

"What things?"

"Money, for instance." I indicate the door with a little toss of the head, which upsets her even further.

"Young man," she says, "let me hear no more of this. Whenever even the most perfectly unselfish gesture is pre-formed for the benefit of society, mercenary and sadistic motives are popularly ascribed to it. This has been my ex-perience. Mistrust. We no longer believe in the goodness of our fellow-men. Do you know, Bodkin, I have even heard people accuse the staff here of maltreating the boys? Well? And what is one to say? One merely shrugs. I am disap-pointed in you, Bodkin. Now let me go!" Pulling loose desperately, she runs up to her apartment. She's been seven-teen years dabbing the bruises, the witch.

Miss Rose stops at the head of the stairs. "Forgive me," she whispers, out of breath. She glances about furtively and then leans down to me at a precarious angle. "I know about it, my boy, I know. What is one to do, however? Let us be honest about our Miss Rose—let us say precisely now what I am. I am an old woman in a madhouse. What, really, do you expect of me? I am efficient, I do what I was hired to do, and you may thank your lucky stars that I am as I am. I am not the serpent and the eagle, Bodkin, only their hand-maid. One ounce of iodine in these bony old hands of mine will destroy more dragons in one instant than the sum total of intuitions and righteous gossip conceived by me in the whole of my seventy-one years on this planet. Gossip . . . yes, I leave that to you, my boy. I know Weasel is a mon-ster, I know what he does with those boys. A bit of the roughhouse—ah well, it hurts no one, really. You're far worse than Weasel, Bodkin. Why aren't you at your post now, eh? A slap in the face, a fearsome stroke in the nastier regions—it's the only sort of joy for these people—for all of us, in fact. And as for the money? The scramble is worth watching; it provides us with amusement, it keeps things moving, and movement is life. And life . . . you're on the wrong track, you and your friends over there. You and your Boober, that gloomy fool. Why they've kept him on, I'll never understand. A regular saint he is. Phooey! I don't think he bathes."

There are footsteps coming to the door. We never heard the safe shut. He is sly, Pincher. Miss Rose is in a fluster. You can see in her eyes she doesn't want to be the one to catch him, that it would be a greater disgrace for her to catch Pincher with his abomination showing than for her to be caught herself. It's an idea she has, I suppose—that no one is quite as wretched as herself. She doesn't want it refuted either, at this late date. She is horrified and makes for her door, but it jams, and Pincher is already out of the office, trying to find something decent to do with his hands. She ventures a glance at him, then manages the lock and bolts into her apartment.

But "Miss Rose," Pincher says before she has had a chance to shut the door. "A little word with you, dear."

She reappears, her chin high. "Good morning, Mr. Pincher," she says.

"Up early, I see."

"Yes. I've been out for a bit, getting some air. These rooms are terribly overheated. I've told you time and again. One ought not subject innocent children to such conditions. An intelligent heating system would eliminate sixty to seventy percent of the epidemics and save money in the long run. *Money,* d'you hear? Mark my word—Hippocrates, sir, Galen, Pasteur, Lister; I speak from a mountaintop." She exits with a grand, composed contempt, though she is shaking dreadfully.

Pincher blinks at the space she has just vacated and then

clutches my arm. "I'm so glad you're here, Bodkin. I forgot! The most essential thing!"

"And what's that, Mr. Pincher?"

"The sheets! Dr. Sweeney's idea. I was supposed to tell you first thing . . . and then, you know, I forgot. How could I forget?"

I'd like to clout him one, rifle his pockets right now—and I ought to, just to give him a turn. But he is bigger than me, that's the thing, or else I would have done him in long ago, in the style to which he is accustomed.

"What sheets, Mr. Pincher? I've got to get back to my post."

"Of course. That's the essential thing, to be at your post. There's no denying that to be at one's post at all times is of the first importance. Look at me! Twenty-four hours a day! As if I didn't have enough to do, there I am in the office . . . and what am I doing in there, Bodkin?"

"Mopping the floors."

"Arranging the files! You have no idea of these secretaries, the inefficiency. The entire filing system would go to pieces if I let up for one moment. But that's neither here nor there. I'm not one to blow my own horn. Sacrifice, but silence—that's my motto."

"What about the sheets?"

"You'll be washing them," Pincher says, quite business-like all of a sudden. "That is, you and the others. It's to be the duty of the watchmen from now on to wash and dry the linens in each of their stations once a week. I want you to be the one to tell the others, Bodkin."

"Really, Mr. Pincher, you place too much confidence in me."

"They respect you, my boy. You'll know how to put it to

them. It was Dr. Sweeney's idea, you see. You look unhappy. Don't look unhappy. It's a splendid idea, really. The
doctor is a genius, don't for one moment doubt that! He
believes—as he explained it all to me, in detail—he believes
that this simple chore, which will require only a few hours
of your time a week, will bring the watchmen closer to the
boys, to the day shift, to the entire institution, in fact. 'Even
the resentment,' he says—if you will permit me to quote his
exact words—'Even the *resent*ment which this new chore is
bound to rouse in you, will bring you closer and make you
share, as it were, the overwhelming sense of *futility,* that is
to say, the *despair,* which in fact is at the very root of our
esprit de corps.' Did you ever, Bodkin? The depths of the
man's thought are not to be fathomed, I tell you."

"But there are one hundred and eighty goddamn beds,
Pincher, and just five watchmen . . . I mean, what the hell,
man! Are you out of your mind?"

"I anticipated this . . ." he sighs.

"And what are we supposed to wash them in? The bathtub?"

"Yes. You'll each be provided with a washboard, of
course, in addition. And detergents and bleach, but that
goes without saying."

"And the Industrial Revolution—that goes without saying too, I suppose. Eli Whitney, Benjamin Franklin, Robert
Fulton, Thomas Edison, General Electric, William Bendix
—all without saying. Pincher, better give us a running
brook and let's beat the laundry on the rocks. Tubs and
washboards, that's neither here nor there. If we're going to
go back, then *let's go back!*"

"It's only one night a week, Bodkin. Not so very much to
ask—"

"I suppose you think you'll be saving a fortune on the laundry bill too."

"Money is not the question," Pincher says peremptorily. "It's getting late. I've got to get home and shave. I have to be on duty in less than an hour. Meanwhile, I suggest you get busy and inform the others."

He goes out the door, and I follow him across the courtyard.

THE INTRUDER

We part company at the flagpole. He walks away toward his car in the trees. His breath trails back over his right shoulder. I collect Weasel and take him over to Boober's sitting room. Boober is there; he's good at taking hints. He looks for the sign in all things. It is very bright, his room. Trembley and Ashe show up too, straightway. They never miss a trick.

I play the mystery a bit to settle everyone down, and then I let them have it neat, the whole banality. Weasel smiles; he seems pleased. Trembley and Ashe both look to Boober, who just sits, his eyes gushing, bulging out of his head; his arms are stretched out, his hands clutching his knees.

"But . . . they *mic*turate on them," he says at last. He's incredulous and hoarse. "I mean, Bodkin, he can't actually expect . . . perhaps you misunderstood."

"What's wrong, Boober?" says Weasel. "It's not so hard to believe. It'll be good for you. It's about time you did something to earn your money." He sneers. He has awfully thin lips for a black man.

Miss Rose appears in the doorway. She has let her hair down, and it is not a pretty sight. She's come out without her coat this time. The light doesn't do much for her flannel gown. It was white once, but yellow now, and the huge flowers that were printed on it—how long ago? a thousand years—have with exception of the thorns faded almost entirely.

Boober puts his face in his hands and sobs. Weasel crosses his legs, lights a cigarette and lets the smoke curl up out of his nose. Trembley and Ashe turn away and face their respective corners.

"Hi, Miss Rose," I say.

But she doesn't acknowledge me. She stares at the monkish bald spot on the crown of Boober's head. "Somebody is ill here," she says. "Is that correct, Boober? Look at me, idiot. Somebody is ill. Who is it? Show him to me."

Boober looks up at her and nods. "Yes," he says, "somebody is ill."

Boober takes things in a misty, crooked way, and therefore quite without malice, gets life moving into surreptitious passages.

"It's Group Eight!" she cries. "Isn't it? I knew it! Why didn't someone come and tell me? Don't you care? Those poor children could drop dead and you wouldn't lift a finger, Boober. Well? And what are you weeping about night and day? Has somebody hurt your feelings? Too bad! Who is it, Boober? Show him to me at once! Who is ill?"

"Everyone," he says.

"Ah God, the whole group? Is it the plague then, man? I had a premonition that that's what it was." She raises a thermometer in the air didactically: "The Black Death, gentlemen."

Weasel doesn't take kindly to this idea of the Black Death. He has an overactive sense of metaphor, and takes her to mean something unsociable. He stands up and puts his thumbs in his belt. One ought to give him a few lessons in history, some of the basic facts, and then maybe he wouldn't take things so personally all the time. No perspective, that's Weasel. He looks to Ashe, the only other Negro present, for a little brotherly support for his indignation, but the whole business is lost on Ashe, who takes everything on one plane and anyway hasn't heard a thing that's been said. He is praying.

Miss Rose brushes past Weasel into the hallway that leads to Group Eight, her gown billowing about her, her hair flying. I take her arm to stop her and get things ironed out, but she shakes me off. Nobody else seems to care. She has a head start. The arm I grabbed was already going a mile a minute getting the mercury in the thermometer down, and it is still going as she vanishes into the darkness at the end of the hall. I follow her. She has flicked her flashlight on and is ducking frantically in and out among the double-decker beds, from boy to boy. Nobody wakes; she has the touch. She feels the foreheads, one by one, and then the wrists, counting over them silently with her lips. She never does use the thermometer. They are cool as cucumbers, aloft, beyond her fears, in a better world. It's insulting.

Miss Rose flies back to the sitting room, with me at her heels. "You're trying to make a fool of me, Boober!" she cries. "I won't stand for it! Won't!"

"It is not, unfortunately, in my power to make either a fool or a sage of another human being," says Boober. "If you feel, however, that you have been made a fool of, Miss Rose—which sentiment, I assure you, I do not share—then you have only yourself to blame. One is the maker of one's own foolishness."

"You deliberately lied to me. For your own amusement."

"Not at all—"

"Nobody is sick in Group Eight!"

"Everybody is sick in Group Eight, Miss Rose."

"D'you hear, Bodkin? D'you see what he is trying to do to me?"

"There, there," I say, and go to her.

"Don't touch me!" She shakes her thermometer at me.

Weasel says menacingly, "Who is that Black Death you talking about, Miss Rose? Hum?"

"Eh? What's that?" She looks at him quizzically, then turns to me, and pointing her thumb sideways, says, "What's he say? Is the man ill?"

"Yes, he is ill," says Boober. "And you too, Miss Rose, are ill. Quite ill."

Which decidedly is not what is called for. They're at her from all sides. People say what is on their minds, every time.

Her eyes open wide at Boober, as if she would devour him with them. "What's that you say? Ill? Me? A pox on you, man! I'll make you choke on those words—"

"They have choked me quite sufficiently already, my dear."

"D'you hear, Bodkin? The man's mad as a hatter. His tongue ought to be cut out of his throat!"

"And now, of all things, lads," says Trembley, with a sad lilt of his bottle, "Pincher wants us to wash the sheets."

Weasel chuckles, touches Trembley on the shoulder affectionately, takes the bottle, wets his lips to show his humor, and returns it. That's nice of Weasel; I like that. Miss Rose darts her eyes about; she can't make head nor tail of this crew. Someone is moving about upstairs. Who's that? Everybody looks up save Boober, who is beyond mortal surprises. Somebody up there is big, with heavy shoes. It isn't one of the boys. But everyone is here! One must investigate; there is little else to do in such cases; all the rest comes to idle speculation and sickly dreams. But Boober won't go, and it is his group—we have a code among us to respect the authority of each watchman over his own quarters.

"But maybe it's a thief, Boober," I say. "You ought to go up and have a look at least. It's in your own interest. What if something happens? They'll fire you. Come on, old friend, go on up and have a look. I'll go with you if you like."

"Whatever goes up," Boober says, "must come down," and he indicates the passage to the stairs. If anyone is up there, he will have to come that way and pass through the sitting room.

"You didn't see him go up, did you?" I say.

"No—"

"Well then, what makes you think you'll see him come down?"

"Nothing. But in that case, there's nothing to fear. For

the intruder would be invisible, a phantom, and I am certainly not any use against a phantom—true?—and therefore cannot be held responsible. You, Bodkin, of course, would have me engage him in combat, for you are greatly fond of quixotic spectacles. But the administration, I assure you, does not share your tastes in entertainment. No, if anything is liable to have me fired, it is my going up that staircase. Besides, very likely it is not a phantom at all, but a quite ordinary person who slipped through here while I was out visiting you."

"If you're not going up," says Miss Rose, "then I am. You're all of you despicable."

But as she heads for the passage, in comes Pincher, bringing the cold along with him.

"Ah, Miss Rose," he says. "Up and about again, I see."

She stops, exasperated, then turns around slowly and glares at him. "One does grow weary of your appearing and disappearing, Mr. Pincher. Why aren't you home in bed now, eh? Must you be poking your nose ever and anon into affairs which do not concern you? It is enough to drive one batty. 'Up and about again'? Yes, I am up and about again. Furthermore, it is no business of yours how high I am up or what I am about. You have no authority whatsoever over me. I pay allegiance to no one but Hippocrates, sir, and his noble descendants."

"My, my," says Pincher. "You *are* overwrought, aren't you. I think what you need is a nice long vacation, a trip abroad perhaps, and also, if you don't mind my saying so, an appointment with a competent beautician."

Miss Rose touches her hair, her eyes fill up, her lips tremble; she flings the thermometer against the wall and runs by Pincher, out into the air. Mercury dances on the floor. I go after her and catch up with her in the courtyard, but she waves me away grievously, her head down, her hands up, and disappears into her quarters.

When I return to the sitting room, I find a noisy affair, Pincher and Boober raising Cain, Weasel muttering about something or other, Trembley moaning in his brew, and Ashe exhorting heaven's witness.

"There is nothing, furthermore," Boober is saying, "nothing of the kind, Mr. Pincher, stated in the contract."

"Contract! What contract?"

"I happen to have a duplicate with me. Would you care to see it? I carry it about with me at all times. It is rather old, of course, yellow and frayed, but valid nonetheless."

He reaches into the breast pocket of his coat, but Pincher will have none of that; he shakes his head with sincere disgust. "What do I care for your contracts, Boober?"

"Nothing, obviously. But to me, sir, it is an agreement at once binding and profound. And I assure you, that in the clause which specifies the duties I am obliged to perform, there is no mention of laundering sheets or other menial labors."

"Then we'll draw up a new contract. What do you think of that?"

"I think nothing at all of it, sir, with all due respect to yourself. I won't sign."

"I shall order you to sign, Boober."

"Order away, Mr. Pincher. I stand firm upon the immutability of the already existing agreement."

"You'll disobey?"

"I will."

"Good. I'll fire you on the grounds of your willful disobedience. Take special note, Boober, of the insubordination clause."

"I have already, Mr. Pincher, thank you. Wherein is stated that the employee may immediately be discharged upon failing, at the request of his superiors, to perform any duty whatsoever within reason."

"Just so."

"I hardly think it within reason, however, that for faithfully refusing to usurp a certain contract, one may be discharged according to any clause in the said contract itself. This is clearly absurd, and a very odd use of reason indeed."

"The uses of reason, Mr. Boober, are many."

"So too, sir, are the *abuses!*"

I take advantage of the confusion and slip by, unnoticed, up to Group Eight to investigate, in homage to Miss Rose, the intruder that everyone seems to have forgot. But he's not here any more. Where has he got to? There isn't a sound, a trace of him. It could be he slipped through the sitting room unnoticed, just as I did.

When I return, Pincher is at the door, shaking his fist. "We'll see about it! We'll just see, Boober!" And then he is gone.

Weasel pulls up his chair to confront Boober squarely. "I know why you won't wash the linens, Boober," he says. His lips quiver; he is in a rage inside. Self-control comes harder to him than most people, but he makes a noble effort. He forces his voice to a whisper.

"Ah, Weasel, Weasel," says Boober.

"Don't 'Weasel' me, Boober. I don't want to hear. I know you, I know. You are a sick man. I won't hear you any more. You make a death in my soul. And you hate me. Oh, how you hate me. And you hate these little boys. Be-

cause you are white and they black. No, no, don't say no—
because I see it. See? I see it! You look at them and I see
you see them bound in chains. But they are not in chains.
They have broke free. And they have the chains in their
hands, and they have made a heavy weapon of the chains,
Boober. They are going to kill you, just wait, with your own
chains. You wait. I pray every minute that these little boys
here won't forget the nigger in their souls. The *nigger—
that's* what knows about *chains.*"

"Stop, Weasel!" cries Ashe. "Can't you see how the man
weeps?"

"What's that you say, nigger? He weeps? He weeps? Yes,
you'd best weep, white man. Over those terrible mistakes
you made, because those mistakes are going to come up and
make an even bigger mistake out of you. And oh, what a
terrible, sorrowful mistake you are going to be, Boober.
They going to kill you—slow."

"I guess that's about enough, Weasel," I say.

But he won't turn to me. He talks to Boober. "Who's
that? Is that the Jew, Boober? Yes, I think that was the Jew
spoke. I don't like him neither. He's a nigger, that Jew.
They all niggers, those Jews. They are the lost tribe of
niggers. We took them out in the woods one day and lost
them. We didn't want them no more. Sickly—they weren't
black enough. And they all had hair in their noses. And if
there's one thing we niggers can't bide by, it's a man with
hair in his nose. It's not dignified. Dignity, see, that's important to us niggers. That's why we want you to help us wash
the smell out of our bedsheets. See? But you don't want to
help us. Why? Because then you can't have *your* dignity any
more. Because *you* can't be dignified 'less *I* am *un*dignified. Also, you are lazy, man, and no count."

"Let him be, Weasel—"

"And you smell bad. And you drink too much. And you are superstitious. And oversexed. In fact, you just like a nigger except you ain't black. And a nigger that's not black isn't anything better than a Jew. But you not even a Jew, Boober. You zero. A vale of tears, that's all, and the shadow of death himself. We don't need kill you, come to think of it, because you're dead a long time past."

"Most inappropriate," says Ashe. "Pay him no mind, Boober."

"Oh, and you don't like Pincher, do you, dead man. But *I* like Pincher—listen to me!—because he knows how to move them white pieces around the board, and he going to make sure there's plenty room for the black ones to get through. And we're going to get lots of kings, you know it. All kings—black kings, Boober, on the white squares. And you're going to be off the board, down there on your hands and knees on the sidelines, and not weeping neither, but sweating blood, man, and doing the imperial goddamn laundry!"

"Enough!" cries Ashe. "Get down on your knees, brother, and beg the Lord's forgiveness at once for abusing this perfect man. Boober is just, Weasel, and merciful, and loves every living creature. What do you think makes him weep without let? Is it hate? Come now, does he hate you?"

"You know something, Ashe?" says Weasel, narrowing his eyes. "You black, but you're no nigger. You're a dirty snowbird."

"May God forgive you, friend. What you say comes out of nowhere. Who has mentioned black and white till now? One wonders what dialogue your brain makes of the plain speech the rest of us hear. God knows. As for my part, I think only this, that there is less of malice in you than of madness—"

"No, Ashe," says Boober, "he is right."

"No he's not," says Trembley, sucking his teeth and leaning back in his chair, "because Ashe isn't any kind of a
snowbird. I know him well enough, and he's a dirty old
nigger through and through."

"And you're a no-count boozer," says Weasel. "A sot, a
white sponge—"

"No, listen to me," says Boober. "Weasel is right. He
speaks the truth, Ashe. Inside me is a great evil. It is not *he*
who ought to beg forgiveness of *me,* but *I* who ought—"

"What do you mean I'm a white sponge?" says
Trembley.

"You heard The Weeper, didn't you?" says Weasel. "He
says I speak the truth. Well? And so I do. I speak the truth.
And you're an Irish kike, Trembley, a Mickey Jew—"

"No, no, gentlemen. Listen to me, please," says Boober.
"Just one moment. Let me open my soul to you, and in an
honest confession once and for all make a clean breast of
the multitude of horrors—"

"I'm not Irish," says Trembley, "I'm Welsh, and let me
tell you—"

"Who gives a difference?" says Weasel, "Irish, Welsh, it
all boils down to rotten potatoes."

"You've gone too far," says Trembley as he rises up and
waltzes his bottle before us. "I take this as an insult to my
grandfather. And he, lads, was a man. He was—"

"He was an Irish pickle is what he was." says Weasel.
"He immigrate in a barrel, I bet you, because he too cheap
to buy a goddamn—"

"Gentlemen, gentlemen!" cries Boober. He throws his
arms out, as if attempting to embrace all the yammer at
once, but his arms are short. He says, "Allow me but a
moment to speak. I feel the need to speak so pressing . . . so

very pressing. I feel I should like to expose naked before you—one moment!—that which is petty, evil and barbarous in my soul—wait, please—so that you may see in it as you see in a mirror that which lies hidden perhaps within your own souls, and in the souls of all men—of the living and the dead, and of those yet to be born. For in this way—"

"There was nothing evil," says Trembley, "in my grandfather's soul. If you're going to speak of humanity in that fashion, lad, pray let's understand first off that my grandfather's to be excluded from the discussion."

"Your grandfather, your grandfather," says Weasel.

"The attitude you take toward Trembley's grandfather," says Ashe, "is much to be deplored. I know; I met the man. On his deathbed, Weasel. He was a priest, a man of the highest principles, who suffered all his life from ignominious persecutions—"

"Please," says Boober, but he is hoarse, and whipped, and has his head in his hands, and his elbows on his knees. "One word, one word—"

I leave. It is cold; the air picks me up. We have a half-hour to go, and I like to tie up the loose ends before the day shift arrives. Besides, it is important to make a show of diligence during this last half-hour if you want to keep your nose clean. The other fellows will follow suit in a minute or two; all of them know the time of day. In fact, they are unanimously agreed on it.

Miss Rose flies out into the courtyard, in just a nightgown and her bare feet. Propriety won't put up with her very much longer. She is coming out of Ashe's quarters. I call after her, but she is in a fit to get back to her place and won't stop. Like an angel she looks from where I stand, a mere nightgown sailing before the wind; a bit of gilt from the horizon puts an edge on her wings. She spins around in her doorway and wails, "Premonitions again, Bodkin. Group Thirteen, Ashe's quarters. But it was nothing, nothing. I'll catch my death—"

She disappears and I go on to my place, where there is peace and quiet. I'll make a quick bed check. I have three floors to watch: the hold, the deck and the crow's-nest. Like Weasel, I get carried away with metaphors. A dangerous inclination, but it gives me an original slant and the night slides down easier. Each watchman is responsible for one ward. There are three groups in a ward, and twelve boys in a group. The boys range in age from seven to thirteen, most of them Negroes, some whites and some mulattoes. The red and yellow races are not represented. I am in charge of Group One on the first floor, Two on the second, and Three on the third—a very orderly arrangement. All is quiet on the first floor.

There is a shuffle on the second, but that is Blinken and Nod, nothing to bother your head about. They are going at it in the utility closet, rattling the cans. They make a touch of love before sunrise to get their appetites up. I tap three times on the door, and each of them whispers "Okay" through the keyhole. We've reached an understanding, the three of us, and so long as it is kept mum and doesn't get out of hand, till envy gets the better of me we'll let nature take her devious course. They have known each other since the streets, and I don't like to break up a friendship. What for?

I go on up to the third floor, which is dark except for one shaft of pale light from the window. In the far corner of the room is a man; he says my name as though it were a question, and I answer yes; then he moves near the window. It is Director Doberman, and he has a boy cradled in his arms. The boy doesn't seem to be breathing, though his mouth is open slightly. I think it is Page—Benjamin Page— one of the boys in Group Three. Doberman asks me where I have been.

"Well," I say, "I've been over in the other wing with Boober and the other fellows. I was telling them about the sheet business. Pincher's idea. And Dr. Sweeney's. You must have arrived only a few minutes ago, because I was just—"

"I've been waiting here for hours, Bodkin," he says— which for some reason amuses me.

"I'd have gone to look for you, and I almost did," he continues, "but then I thought better of it. I thought: I'll wait for him, I'll hold the boy in my arms and wait. I didn't expect you to be so long. I had wanted only to teach you a simple lesson, you see."

I try to get a better look at the boy. "That's Page, isn't it?" I say.

Doberman answers yes, that it is Page, and adds that the boy has been dead for several hours. He says this in a sad, calm voice and looks at me coldly. He appears to derive some satisfaction out of observing the effect his words have on me. But this is a perverse kind of satisfaction; I don't like it; my hands are trembling and I put them in my pockets.

I say, "It's odd that nobody saw you slip in tonight."

"I parked my car in the woods. I came up the back by the fire escape. I had intended to look around. I've been worried of late . . . the attempts on my life. This, however, is what I discovered. You would have discovered the boy yourself, of course, eventually. But you didn't. I did. Do you see? *I* did. I've been overconcerned about my welfare, Bodkin."

I am uneasy. Doberman is looking specially pathetic to-night. He used to keep up an elegant appearance, until the first attempt on his life a few months ago. Now he neglects his clothes, his hair, his fingernails and his shaving habits. He has even developed a mildly offensive odor, which is the occasion of some humor among the staff. Also, he has taken to writing about himself. He is recording in a finicky old-fashioned prose the history of his unhappiness—and enjoying it, I would say. I have felt uncomfortable in his presence ever since he began to show me these literary efforts of his.

"Bodkin, Bodkin!"

That is Boober's voice, from outside, and other voices in a great muddle join in. I go to the window. Weasel, Ashe, Trembley and The Weeper are marching across the court-yard. They have someone else with them: an old man in shabby dress, unmistakably a tramp. He is of a type we come across here two or three times each winter—huddled up in a corner, asleep, barefoot, with his head on his shoes, wanting nothing more than shelter for the night. We are in the habit of making a fuss over these poor birds; we really celebrate their arrival, in fact. Each one is a welcome diver-sion. We'll give him excellent advice, a cup of coffee for the road and throw him back to the night with howls of execration.

"It's the watchmen," I say to Doberman. He hasn't heard me, I think.

"Bodkin, Bodkin!" Boober again. They are into the vestibule on the first floor, my buddies; their voices echo in the halls.

"We have discovered the intruder!" cries Ashe.

"Bodkin, where are you?" cries Trembley.

"Don't be so rough with the poor man, Weasel," says Boober.

"Poor man, poor man. I'll give him a poor man, all right."

"My throat," says a strange voice—the tramp, I suppose.

"Not so tightly, Weasel," says Ashe.

"Where is that Bodkin?" says Boober.

"You're choking me. I can't breathe," says the tramp.

"What do we need that Jew bastard for, anyway?" says Weasel. "He probably asleep in one of the empty beds. Let's just call the cops."

"In the first place," says Boober, "there are no empty beds—"

"And in the second place," says Ashe. "I cannot permit you to insult the religion of my friend Bodkin in my presence. By my silence, Mr. Weasel, I would indicate agreement, and I feel it my duty—"

"Your duty, your duty."

"To *inform* you that an insult to my friend is an insult to me."

"My throat!" says the tramp.

"Shut up," says Weasel.

"Don't you understand what is going on here, Bodkin?" says Doberman, and his voice, demented suddenly, sounds as if it is coming from as far away as the others.

"Are we just going to stand here or what?" says Weasel.

"Somebody ought to go look for Bodkin," says Trembley.

"I'll go," says Ashe.

"Never mind," says Weasel. "I'll go. You creeps just hold on to the good brother here. I mean *tight*. Bodkin! Where the hell are you, man?" He is coming up the stairs two at a time.

What's that? Cans and bodies knocking against the boards down there.

"Look here now what I found," says Weasel. He laughs.

"We wasn't doing nothing!" That's Blinken. His voice quivers.

"Guess what I found up here in the closet, gentlemen?" shouts Weasel from the second landing.

"What did you find, Weasel?" says Trembley.

"I found two lovers. Ha, ha, Blinken and Nod."

"We're no lovers!" says Nod. "You let me go, you nigger."

"Now, now, son. D'you hear that, gentlemen? This little black boy calls *me* a nigger. That's good, boy."

"I ain't no boy neither."

"And what's that make you, boy, if I am a nigger?"

"That doesn't make me nothing. I'm a nigger too, yeah— so what! But you're a blacker nigger than me."

"No, you're no nigger," says Weasel. "You just a little fairy—ow! I'll teach you to bite Weasel. I'll bite your—hey! You come back here!"

"Mr. Bodkin, Mr. Bodkin!" cries Nod.

He is running up the stairs. I don't hear Weasel come after him; probably he is holding on to Blinken, a bird in the hand. Then I hear him go back downstairs, and topical debate ensues on the ground floor.

Eyes open in the double-decker beds, but nobody sits up or gets out. Most of the boys clap their pillows over their heads and press them against their ears, or crawl deeper into the blankets. Doberman retreats into the dark corner.

Nod appears; he is breathing heavily, in a highly nervous state, and has a little scratch running down from the corner of his eye.

"You done a mean trick, Mr. Bodkin," he says. "You promised nobody would beat on me when you was on duty. How come you said that and then let that faggit loose and never give me and Blinken a word to let on? I'm little and skinny, that's why. But I'm going to get big, you wait. I'm going to write to my brother too. He's in the Golden Gloves. You wait. One, two, three, he knock everybody out up here. Oh, there's going to be some bloody faces—"

"Get a grip on yourself, Nod," I say. "Remember? You don't have any brother. You admitted it yourself the other day. I was really getting some hope up for you. You know that's crazy. Don't you now? Because the sooner you stop saying crazy things, the sooner—"

"I *do* got a brother. And he has golden gloves too—don't you make no mistake about it. Solid gold, Mr. Bodkin— Hey, who's that? Is that you, Mr. Doberman?" He squints; his eyes aren't yet accustomed to the light outside the closet.

Nod stiffens and walks cautiously toward Doberman.

"What is the meaning of this?" cries Miss Rose. Now she too is down there in the vestibule. I wonder if she is still in her nightgown. She says, "Is that a way to treat the aged? Have you lost your minds completely? Let him go, I say. At once. This is a disgrace."

"Who do you have in your arms there, Mr. Doberman?" says Nod.

"You don't understand, Miss Rose," says Ashe. "I would

be the last to abuse the aged. This man, old as he is, is hardly to be handled delicately, however. Likely he has stolen, likely he has committed many a heinous crime, mayhap he is a lunatic. Mr. Trembley found him muttering in the water closet."

"The poor man!" she cries. "Get him a cup of coffee or something, why don't you? You idiots! What are you doing with that child, Mr. Weasel?"

"Entertaining him, Miss Rose."

"He hardly seems amused. I don't like it. And as for you, you poor old fool, what do you have to say for yourself? Are you a lunatic, truly? It is certain, at any rate, that you are a trespasser. Well? Speak up."

"My throat. I, I . . ."

"It's Page," says Nod. He touches the hand, the face, the mouth. He says, "You know what? Page is dead, Mr. Bodkin." A smile breaks out on his face, but something gets the better of him and he forces his lips together and frowns as best he can. He looks up at Doberman. "How come he's dead like that?" he says. "Have you been beating on him, Mr. Doberman? My brother always said look out for you. He said, 'Doberman he keeps his hands in his pockets. And a man that keeps his hands in his pockets don't hit you. He don't want to hit you. He wants to kill you.' Now you done what you want. Oh, you're bad. Kill me too, why don't you."

"Doberman didn't kill Page," I say. "He merely discovered the body—that is a distinction you ought to make, Nod."

But Nod doesn't catch my meaning; I've never been able to get through to him. Maybe he didn't hear me, though. Maybe I just thought it without saying it; I can't ever be sure. He is shrieking uncontrollably at me and Doberman.

This brings the sleepers out of their beds. All of them are awake now, it seems. They are rising in all the wards, gathering in a mob and running up from the first and second floors and the other wing.

They are talking all at once, as they rush in from the staircases and the corridors.

"Doberman slit his throat."

"No, no, the Page ain't cut."

"He give him poison, I bet you."

"Let me see, I can't see."

"We're going to kill you, Mr. Doberman."

"White man."

"We got him outnumbered, don't we?"

"What're we waiting for, then?"

"Till he kills us too, that's what we're waiting for."

"A lot of skinny little boys make a big strong man."

"That's right, that's right!"

"I'm afraid."

"Who is that afraid?"

"Nobody."

"Nobody afraid, man."

"Out of my way, out of my way!" Boober's voice is heard, and his large unhappy person barrels through the mob, the hair at the side of his head sticking out in all directions. He's in a sweat, swelled up so, he can't contain himself.

"What's this?" he says. "You think Mr. Doberman could do such a thing? Shame on you. I, Mr. Boober, am the murderer. And if you don't get control of yourselves, Mr. Boober is going to kill you too. With my bare hands. Do you see these hands? Eh?"

"Booby," says Nod, "you couldn't kill anybody. You're so fat you can't hardly move. *We're* going to kill *you* though. Right?"

"Right, right!"

"And the Jew too."

"He's so quiet, that Jew."

"He thinks if he's quiet, we'll forget about him."

"But we don't forget, no sir."

"He shakes. Look at Bodykin shake, ha, ha—"

"And I'm shaking too. So you look out." That's Weasel. He has Nod by the throat, lifts him off the floor and smacks him across the face I don't know how many times, up high, so that everyone can see. They see. They back down and give us room.

"You get downstairs, all of you," says Weasel breathlessly. He throws Nod back into the crowd and raises one bony fist, his eyes shining. "Have you no respect for the dead? Were you brung up in a jungle? Mr. Doberman will send you back to Africa he sees you behave like cannibals. That is why you are here, see? You are all savages. And lunatics. You don't know how to live among civilized peoples. What will your mamas and papas and brothers and sisters say when I write and tell them how you behaved? Mr. Weasel he is going to write letters—wait and see. About all of you that's here. Mr. Weasel he is always watching you, and don't you forget it."

"But Director Doberman killed the Page, Mr. Weasel."

"That's a funny idea you got there, boy, but I got an even funnier one. Listen here. *My* idea is one of you lunatic *chil*dren is the killer what done in the poor little Page in his sleep. What do you think of that? Hum? Christ have mercy on your souls, children, when Mr. Weasel gets his back up. He is an angry god that does not rest till justice do!"

I look out the window. The station wagon pulls up front. It has brought the Days from the staff house at the top of the hill. They pile out in a fit, like fire fighters, red with the cold, but they can't get up the stairs because everybody else is coming down. The boys are making the best of a defeat they're not sure they regret, weeping here and there and horsing it up to make even the descent of the dismal stairway give a lift to their spirits. I, Boober, Weasel, Doberman and Page are left alone.

"Thanks, Weasel," I say.

He grunts.

The day shift takes matters in hand in the courtyard. They assemble the boys in their tattered pajamas and bare feet in the snow; teeth are chattering, and you can hear them from up here with the windows closed.

Miss Rose runs up and down the ranks. She lectures at the Days, but they stick to their guns, and so she appeals to Pincher, who seems to have just arrived. He has assumed generalship straight off, and a heavy concentration; he bears the stamp of a great leader.

"They'll catch pneumonia!" cries Miss Rose. "Take them in. I'll have you up before the authorities, Mr. Pincher."

"I am the authority," he says.

She is decked out in her expansive starchy whites and her hat with the two peaks. I don't think she knows about Page; she would be up here by now.

On the floor beside Page's bed lies a small notepad. I pick it up unnoticed and try to read by the light from the window. It is Doberman's handwriting: egotistical capitals and lines that slant downward at a sad angle. I won't have time to read much of it, but I can see at once that it is a meditation, full of cloudy self-recriminations, on the subject of Page's death. He lied to me; he had not been standing with Page in his arms the whole time; he had been writing. One can't write with a child in one's arms. I slip the notepad in Doberman's pocket—on the sly, so that Weasel and Boober don't see it—and wink at him. He is startled, looks at me guiltily and says nothing. He starts down the stairs; Weasel, Boober and I follow.

It is not a happy procession, but we make the best of a bad game till we're outside. There the wind smarts my eyes and I have splendid tears, just like Boober's capable of.

Here is Pincher, however, with a felicitous diversion. He has lined up his one hundred and eighty barefoot ragamuffins in two files, between which Doberman is apparently to walk, from my wing to his, saluted on both sides with a fanfare of coughs and sneezes.

Miss Rose clutches Pincher's arm and belabors it to some purpose, but he is transcendent. "Have you no respect for the dead, Miss Rose?" he says, and smiles proudly across the yard at Doberman.

"What do I care for the dead?" cries Miss Rose. "And what are you talking about, anyway? What dead? In a few years I'll have the whole of eternity to show respect for the dead. The living are what concern me now, Mr. Pincher. These poor little children, God help them . . . what are you thinking of? Go inside, children, go. Miss Rose will take the responsibility. Nobody will punish you."

But they stand fast.

"Send them indoors, Mr. Pincher," says Doberman.

Pincher's pride is wounded. "I only thought, sir, that it would improve their sensibilities, that this tribute—which they themselves would pay and, as it were, actively participate in—this tribute to their dead companion would inspire them with awe, and respect for the tragedy, the mystery of human—"

"I shall count to ten, Mr. Pincher. If one living child remains in this courtyard when I have finished, I shall see to it that you are not only dismissed at once, but that you are never again employed in any institution of child welfare in this state, in this country, in the entire—"

"Dismissed, dismissed! Into the building. On the double, now. That's it. D'you hear? Get along there, Nod—what are you staring at?"

Along·with the Days, Pincher runs here and there and encourages the slowpokes. Miss Rose swoops up the smallest of the flock and disappears with him into Boober's quarters.

Doberman counts slowly. By the time he has reached ten, they're all in and the yard is empty, except for us watchmen, Doberman, Page, poor Pincher—and Nod, who, sitting in the snow, his arms and legs crossed, says, "You're out of a job, Mr. Pincher. Because I am a living child."

He turns to Doberman and smiles. Pincher is beside himself.

"Pick him up off the snow, Mr. Weasel," says Doberman, "and wrap him in your coat. I have a word to say to the boy. There you go, son. Are you warm now?"

"Yes, sir."

"Thank you, Mr. Weasel."

"You're welcome, sir."

"Son—listen to me now, carefully. Mr. Pincher is only a human being. Just like you and me. I said I would count to ten—"

"That's right."

"And I did, and he did his best to do what he was supposed to do before I finished."

"But his best ain't good enough."

"True."

"So he's fired."

"No, he is not fired. Since he did his best, and since his best is not good enough, I have to give him a small allowance, to make his best *be* enough. Do you understand?"

"Yeah, I understand. You're a goddamn liar, like everybody else around here. I did my best too. I sat in the snow and nearly froze to death to get that monkey fired."

"I know you did your best, Nod. The trouble is that you did your best to do something bad, and Mr. Pincher did his best to do something good."

"Who says? You think it's something bad I did, to try and get that terrible man out of my sight forever? Well, you just ask one hundred eighty skinny little boys how bad *they* think it is. You ask them. They'll tell you how bad. 'Good' is what they'll tell you. That is one hundred eighty to one. This is a mockracy, isn't it? A free country, yeah."

Doberman shuts his eyes. "Take him to his quarters, Mr. Weasel."

He does, leaves him in the doorway and walks back to us, with Nod shouting at his back. "Yeah, yeah, faggit. *I'm* going to write some letters *too*. To my brother. There'll be retribution—wait and see. You're in cahoots with that big white liar over there, *I* know. That killed the Page. He wants to kill all of us. With his lies. And his bad breath. But he ain't, he ain't!"

One of the Days drags Nod back into the passage, and out comes Miss Rose from the same door.

"Is it true, then?" she cries. "I didn't know—" She stops before Doberman and touches Page's temples, an old habit.

"I had better be taking him away now," says Doberman.

"Let me touch him," she says.

"You're tired, Miss Rose. Take the morning off. Go on, now."

"No, no, wait. I can't. The poor child."

"Forgive us, Miss Rose," says Ashe, coming to her side, his hands clasped before him.

"Eh?" She eyes him distrustfully.

'We should have taken you more seriously."

"What's that?"

"Last night."

"What do I want to be taken seriously for? I am not a serious person. Let me weep."

"We'll have to be getting along," says Doberman.

"And quickly too," says Miss Rose hoarsely and anxiously, but she holds him back. "D'you see? Because these imbeciles are already beginning to take me *ser*iously. God knows what they will begin to take me next. As if that were a great consolation—that I am to be taken seriously!"

"I did not mean—"

"No, no, Ashe. Be still. I'm not so vain as you would like to think. Now you'll begin perking up your ears, won't you, to all the senilities of frightened old ladies. *That* is what frightens me. Seriously. You're just like that young idiot I knew who cut his throat because a gypsy told him she saw suicide in his life line—simply to *please* the old bag of bones. D'you see? Because she was so serious. Do you think I'm to be tickled pink at how seriously you take me all of a sudden? That this bundle of nerves and blood and possibilities must be covered with dirt forever simply so that you won't ignore me from now on? So that you will treat me with some measure of civility? I am too old for that kind of vanity, you . . . you nigger! God forgive me . . ."

Ashe spreads his arms and beams with genuine compassion. "Have no fear. He will forgive you. Come, let us pray together."

Doberman walks away toward the woods, where his car is, but Miss Rose catches up with him and commences to wrestle him for little Page. "Let him go!" she cries. "Where are you taking him?"

"To the Home."

"What *home?* What do you mean? Are you mad? You no longer have any authority over this boy. This is a medical problem, sir. Do you understand? Nothing is certain yet. What was the cause of his expiration? Well? Have you given him hand to heart, mouth to mouth? Have you pumped him, slapped him, put needles in his arm? I do not know the meaning of resignation, sir. Give him to me. I shall have you reported."

"He has been dead for several hours. Go on back, Miss Rose. You need a rest."

Managing the boy away from him however, she runs back toward the infirmary, but falls face down after the first steps, on top of her burden in the snow. Somebody laughs down from one of the windows, but she doesn't hear it, I think.

"Hey," says Weasel, "where's the old man?"

"The tramp!" says Trembley, slapping his forehead.

"Oh Jesus," says Weasel. "Didn't I tell you creeps to watch him? What's wrong with you, Trembles?"

"It was my fault too," says Ashe. "We were both holding him. But then . . . the confusion—"

While the three of them swap imprecations, I stand here —where should I turn?—as Pincher and Boober gather Miss Rose in their arms and carry her off to the infirmary.

Doberman recovers Page and makes off to the woods, where I can just make out the hood of his car, a green, antique Singer, sticking out of the naked pines. He deposits Page in the back seat, slips in behind the steering wheel, and the car explodes.

A spectral issue floats up out of the Singer and insinuates itself through the trees and into the sky. Weasel, Trembley, Ashe and I run to the rescue.

When we arrive, however, we find everything intact. The smoke leaking from the hood is dissipating, and one can begin to see through it Doberman's unhappy eyes. He seems okay. Weasel proceeds to examine the engine, while the rest of us walk around to Doberman, who says, "It's nothing. I forgot."

Odd.

"Hey," says Weasel, "there's a bomb in here, wired to the ignition."

"I know, I know," says Doberman. "It's nothing. Detach it, Weasel, and bring it to me."

It is a queer little affair, a homemade job. Doberman slips it into the glove compartment. "I'll keep it," he says, "as a souvenir."

"You ought to report this to the police, sir," I say. "These attempts on your life are getting out of hand."

"Don't worry, Bodkin. There's no need. It won't happen again. This is the last, I assure you."

"I don't mean to be impertinent, sir, but how do you know? It's clear these people mean business."

"Just take my word for it."

"Permit me, Mr. Doberman," says Ashe. "Certainly you show remarkable courage in the face of doom. Neverthe-less, it is not courage, I should think, but caution that is necessary at the moment. And if I may be so bold as to suggest—"

"You may not. I know what I am about. I ask you, just for one time in your life, to withhold your compassion and have a little faith—just this once, Mr. Ashe—in my judgment."

"Your word has always been law around here, Mr. Doberman," says Weasel. "It's just that Ashe here, and the rest of us, are worried about you. These people who rig up your ignition are like to have lots more rigging up their sleeve. See? You got to fight them with an even bigger rig than any they got. Like the police, see? Else you going to be done in. And then who will keep poor naked children out of the snow? Nobody, not even the biggest and best blast of judgment in the whole wide world, I tell you that. D'you know why? They deaf. You'd be stupefied, Mr. Doberman, at how much the big ears you see everyplace don't hear."

"Your point is well taken, Mr. Weasel. Thank you. And thanks to all of you. But I assure you, there are subtleties in this case of which you are not aware, and which at the moment I am not at liberty to reveal. But patience. Everything in its proper place."

"There is one subtlety though, lads, that we are aware of," says Trembley, "and of which Mr. Doberman is not. Oughtn't we to tell him?"

"He means the tramp, sir," says Ashe.

"Tramp?"

"Yes, sir. We caught a tramp earlier trespassing Mr. Trembley's quarters. We aren't aware of what his intentions were. We found him muttering in the water closet."

"Oh?"

"We seized him directly, of course—"

"And where is he now?" Doberman waits for an answer, but we all of us avoid his eyes. "Well? Mr. Ashe?"

"He escaped, sir."

"Escaped?"

"In the confusion. Mr. Trembley and I were holding him—with the greatest tenacity, sir!—in the courtyard, but then—"

"Never mind," says Doberman. He rubs his eyes.

We are silent for a minute.

"What do you think we ought to do, sir?" I ask.

"Nothing, for the present. We shall wait for the autopsy."

"And then, sir?" says Ashe.

"And then, Mr. Ashe, we shall see what we shall see."

"What about the Fighting Irish, sir?" says Trembley.

"The football team?"

"No, sir. The police."

"As I've already indicated, I think they are best left out of all this for the time being."

"D'you think that wise, sir?"

"I do not think anything on this earth wise, Mr. Trembley, but least of all, the Fighting Irish."

"They serve their purpose, sir."

"Without a doubt. And perhaps we shall have recourse to them in the end. But for the time being—"

"Do you think the tramp could have been the one who murdered Page?" I ask.

"Who said that Page was murdered?" says Doberman.

"Nobody—"

"Bodkin," he says, looking at me fiercely, "what do *you* think?"

"About what, Mr. Doberman?"
"About anything."
"Anything?"
"Yes."
"That's hard to say."

A BRIEF
HISTORY

Weasel, Boober, Trembley and Ashe skip breakfast. They're hungry, sure. They go off someplace. Into town, I think. Doberman is going to the Home, he said. I'm for bed in the staff house. The snow has let up. It is a foot deep, and the wind shakes it off the boughs. It comes down on your shoulders now and again. The path through the woods is circuitous, with easy ups and downs which make one feel a certified mountaineer. It skirts along a brook, a rapid little jack that breaks up the floes before they get a chance to smother it. Page is everywhere into the landscape, crawling about the branches, peering out from the evergreens. I conjure him up lest he get off too light. I could let him hide himself under the inclemency, but then he would be out of mind. That would be no loss, though. The institution has preserved for posterity the complete story of each inmate's life. Some nights when I'm feeling low I take a small pile of this extraordinary literature from the shelf and whip myself up into an ecstacy over the prose.

Page was a mulatto, neither black nor white, merely a wretched child; one didn't know quite what attitude to take toward him. He was the son of a black prostitute who told him that his father was a white soldier killed in Korea. She came home with a knife in her side one morning about four o'clock. Page had been building a model plane at the kitchen table just before she arrived. He had been waiting up for her. He often waited up for her, but this night the hands of the clock had kept dragging her around the numbers and he had wished her dead once or twice. Then dawn arrived and she stumbled in and fell in a heap on the floor. A fine business. He couldn't fathom it and ran into the hall, shouting for explanations. People rushed out from all the doors in the building. The poor wounded bird of the night was carried off in an ambulance, and the boy was permitted to follow in a neighbor's car, but it was no good; the siren shut off before she was halfway.

Page, however, wouldn't shut off, not even for death halfway. He aggravated the teachers, the deans and the principle of the whole thing. In fact, he became a nuisance. On this everyone was agreed. Therefore, since he no longer had a family to wait up for anyway, except an aunt who was no aunt, he was turned over to welfare which was no welfare, a judge who was no judge, and this place which is no place at all.

Eventually news arrived of the killer's apprehension, conviction and sentence to life everlasting—but Page didn't care. "Your old ma's dead, okay, but the killer got life, didn't he?" The boy was not moved. It was plain pigheadedness and nothing else. If there was ever any gratitude in him, it was rarely sufficient to produce a thank you. If you wanted one bad enough, you had to beat it out of him.

I emerge from the trees into an open field and see him up ahead behind a snowdrift, peering around it and beckoning me, his mouth grim, his eyes fierce. I walk toward him, and he laughs, ascends into the air, stretches his arms, arches, glides—then with one stroke rubs out the horizon, paints it new, much farther back, and with a magnificent lack of appreciation dives off the rim of the earth.

Handy greets me at the staff house, takes my arm and draws me into the parlor.

"I've been waiting for you half an hour," he says.

"I got tied up."

"Where's the other watchmen?"

"In town, I think."

He winks. "Booze?"

"Probably."

"I got a message for you fellows. From Mr. Doberman. He called."

Handy—Hanover Jones—is a Negro who has unseemly scars on his face, even on his eyelids. He is what is called a utility man. He trims the grass and the hedges, shovels the snow—and conveys messages. If there is bad news to be had, he will have it and cut everybody in as gay as a blade. As a rule I try discreetly to avoid him, but he is persistent and catches up with you sooner or later. He also chauffeurs the Days and Nights between staff house and madhouse in

the station wagon. But he is chancy at the wheel, and his
indefatigable good humor is not to be endured by a sensible
man, so I have been making the trip on foot the past three
or four years.

He seems to take a certain pride in the place, and this is
understandable. A graduate himself, he is one of the few
among the alumni who made good. Also, he is rarely in a
situation in which he has to exercise power over the boys,
and they are fond of him. They like a smile from a cata-
strophic face. He is the angel of lawns and motors, an
intimation of the happier world, out there, where there are
no rules, no keepers.

"Doberman's called a meet tonight," Handy says. "Nine
o'clock. He told me to tell you."

"Where is it?"

"In his office. All the watchmen are to be there."

"Who else?"

"The Days on Page's group. Three, isn't it?"

"Yes."

"That's Libby, Dew and Peduza," he says. "I guess it'll
be quite a meet. They are some hot Days, them three. I
wouldn't be surprised if the poor little Page did that terrible
turnabout on his own self just so he wouldn't have to sit
through that incredible triple feature ever again. Hey, Bodkin, d'you want to go to the moving pictures with me this
afternoon? I got the day off."

"No thanks. I need some shut-eye."

"Will you tell the other Nights about the meet for me,
then?"

"Tack up some notes on their doors."

DOBERMAN

It is dark in the room when I awake, getting on to nine o'clock and too late for the evening mess. I accept a sandwich most respectfully from the machine in the parlor and eat on the way.

Once into the woods, I scoop up a handful of snow now and then and toss it in the air; I whistle to myself, or to anything that may care to listen. Surely there must be someone listening, some creature lurking about among the pines.

Coming down the path is a boy. He doesn't see me yet. I can tell by the clothes that he is from the institution, but I can't make out his face. He is a runaway. Suddenly he sees me, and he darts off the path into the woods. I run after him. I must catch him. But why? I wonder. Because the trees are thin and don't provide him with camouflage. Because my legs are longer than his. Because, in short, the odds are against him. I see no other reasons—though, certainly, there may be other reasons.

It's Nod. I catch him by the collar of his coat, and he lets out a few profanities at the Jews, takes my entire race to task, in fact, with a prophetic passion, but he gives up readily enough and we walk on together to the school. We walk slowly. It takes me a long time to catch my breath, and my lungs are burning.

I am glad of the company, but he is sullen and won't speak much.

"It's funny," I say after a while. "You're a big hero now. Why do you want to run away?"

"Sure, big hero," he says scornfully.

"Well, you are."

"Sure."

"It took a lot of courage to sit down in the snow like you did, a lot of imagination."

"Sure."

"And I like how you spoke up to Pincher and never blinked an eye. 'You're out of a job, Mr. Pincher. Because I am a living child.' That was good. I'll bet all of the kids here think so too—right?"

"I don't know what they think," he says sharply. He puts his hands in his pockets and knits his brows. "And I don't care, neither. Let's drop it, all right, Bodkin? I don't feel like talking about it."

He has a paper sack in his hand; I ask him what he has

in it. He mistakes my idle curiosity for something else, and hands me the sack with contempt. Inside is nothing but a pair of dirty blue socks with a faded red stripe running up the side. There are holes in them, and the elastic is worn out.

"I bought them myself in the city before I came here," he explains. "It is the only thing I got in this place what belongs to me."

I return it to him, and we remain silent until we emerge from the woods. There is a wide field of snow between us and the rear of the building.

Nod stops, looks up at me and touches my arm. The sight of the institution seems to have made him lively again. "I'm glad you caught me."

"Oh?"

"I was coming back anyway."

"Sure."

"No joke," he says reassuringly.

"How come you were going to come back?"

"Because of Blinken. I don't like to leave him alone in this crazy place. We are friends. Next time I run, he'll come with me."

"How come you didn't take him this time?"

"I tried, but he scared. I got to talk him into it is all."

"And where will you two go, son?"

"To my brother—where else d'you think?"

"Oh, him," I say. "The one with the golden gloves."

"That's right," he says, smiling at me.

I tell him that he has no brother.

"I do got a brother," he says. "Don't worry about it. Let's just forget it."

"Okay."

"Listen," he says anxiously, clutching my arm, "how about letting me sneak up the fire escape . . . okay? You can watch me. Just don't tell nobody I was running, okay? My counselor he will beat me something terrible for it if he finds out. Please? I promise I'll go right back up there, and they'll never know I was out. Will you?"

"I don't know. I'll let you try and sneak up the fire escape, but I don't know yet whether or not I'm going to tell anyone about you. Go ahead. I'll watch till you're in the window. And no tricks, right?"

"Okay." He starts toward the building slowly, but after the first few steps he stops, then turns around and walks back to me. I look at my watch. I am late for the meeting.

"Mr. Bodkin," he says, "can I ask you a question?"

"Sure."

"Who do you think it was killed Page?"

"Well, the autopsy isn't in yet, but my own opinion is that nobody at all killed him, son."

"How do you mean?"

"I mean that I think he probably just died . . . that he got sick all of a sudden and died."

Nod looks at the ground and shakes his head. He is serious and troubled. "No. You wrong. Doberman done it."

It is a peculiar notion, and I don't know exactly what to answer. I tell him we'll talk about it another time.

But he continues to look up at me fixedly. "Will you answer me one more question?"

"I'll try."

"Do you think *I* done it?"

"Did what?"

"Kill Page."

I would laugh, but he doesn't seem to see the humor in it.

"Of course not," I say. "What ever put such an idea into your head?"

He shrugs his shoulders. "Just one more question and then I'm going, I promise."

"Okay."

"Well, my brother always told me you Jewishes bury your peoples high-class . . . is that right . . . ? How come you smile at me?"

"I don't know."

"Well then, *do* you bury yourself high-class or *don't* you?"

"Sure. When we get the chance to, I guess we do."

He scoops up a handful of the fresh snow and puts some of it in his mouth. "Okay then . . . listen, Bodkin, I got to ask you a favor."

A favor. Sure, why not. In a landscape like this, it would be hard to refuse anybody a favor, even this twelve-year-old outlaw who seems to have ready to hand so many importunities about the Jews. Above us is a sky of that certain blue peculiar to these parts, so like a sheet of carbon paper that it seems there ought to be a clean white sheet on the other side with the message in a different color. The pines are tall and black against the snow. There is no wind. The snow lies quietly. The stars have shut their eyes, and there is not a beast, a bird, an insect in the wood. In short, there is not a thing in sight or earshot to prevent one from doing one's fellow-man a good turn.

"What is it?" I say.

He says, "If anything happen to me—you know, like if I

was to die or something?—could you make sure they bury me proper? Nothing fancy. But like just a rock or a bit of wood with my name on it. 'Here lie William Nod.' Like that, see? Make believe I was a Jewish like you. And one for Blinken too—I mean, in case anything happen to him too. Okay?"

"Okay. But look, what makes you think something is going to happen to you and Blinken?"

"Oh . . . nothing," he says, and he makes a nonchalant gesture with his hand.

"You don't want to talk about it, right?"

"Right. You pretty smart."

"Thanks."

He laughs and as a token of affection punches me in the arm. "You're funny, Bodkin."

"I know."

He knits his brows, as though suddenly he has remembered something painful again. "Hey, d'you know what some of the boys here say?"

"What do they say?"

"They say that Mr. Doberman just dump Page into the ocean."

"They do, do they."

"That's right. In Coney Island. They say it is because the Page have no mama or papa to make sure people treat him right."

"That's not true what they say. Page will get a decent burial. Don't you worry about it, okay?"

He casts his eyes down. "If you say so."

"You don't believe me."

"I don't know."

"Okay," I say.

"Okay."

"Not much else I can tell you, is there."

"No, I guess not. Night, Bodkin."

"Good night, son."

He walks across the wide field of snow. I'll stand by the edge of the wood and watch him till he is safely up the fire escape and through the window.

Last spring, Doberman announced at a staff meeting that he intended to begin a culture program which was to consist of monthly doses of high-class amusement—musicians, actors, odd assortments of lecturers and puppeteers. The first event was a concert in the gymnasium, a brass choir from a music institute not far from here. Basketballs were thrown at them in the middle of the second selection, a Bach chorale, but a small dent in the bell of a French cornet was the extent of the damage and the inmates were quieted promptly. All the same, the musicians were frightened and left at once. One of the trombonists, however, a Negro who seemed amused by the affair, stayed on a while, and Nod struck up a conversation with him.

"They all crazy here. Man, I sure do like the trombone."

The next weekend the trombonist returned with his wife, and they spent an afternoon together with the boy. They came back the next weekend and the weekend after that, and soon it became a regular thing for Nod to look forward to. They would bring him candy or a little game or a comic book. Doberman even let them take him into town to a movie or a ball game. Two months ago they came to see about adoption. Doberman had to tell them that unless they moved to the city, the agency would not approve.

"But we live in a beautiful brick house in Westchester!" they told him. "It would be ideal for the boy."

They were nice. Doberman suffered, but nothing could be done. For six years the marvelously eccentric ruling that foster homes must be in the city has been Doberman's largest bone of contention with the social-welfare people and the board of directors. "The city itself, Bodkin, is the principal evil." He may have a point. Three quarters of the children released from Ulser end up within a year back in the courts. "The other quarter, one must suppose, are more cunning and sprightly on their feet," as Doberman puts it.

"I shall go all out this time," he decided in the case of Nod. "I shall have one victory at least before I leave here."

So he took money out of his own pocket, distributed a bribe here and there, burned up a couple of files, and within five days managed to pull it off. The trombonist was ecstatic, and so was Doberman. For days he walked around the grounds, never once going up to his office, and smiled like a madman. He even laughed a couple of times; I heard him. One afternoon he bought two hundred cups of ice cream and handed them out himself, with a merry vigor, in the gymnasium. He had stepped outside the law, risen above it and triumphed. There would be ice cream for everyone from here on out.

And Nod he was so happy and proud of himself that he abandoned his old friend Blinken, took love and pleasure into his own hands and spent the early hours all by himself, aristocratically, with the blanket pulled over his head.

But then there is Pincher. And Pincher is a law-abiding man. He is also, as he says, "Keeper of the King's Conscience," and therefore must do what he can to keep the royal conscience clear. "I shall have to make sure," he said, "that Director Doberman does not get himself into diffi- cultly with this out-of-the-way adoption." He made a few discreet inquiries, a memorandum, a telephone call, and that finished it off quite professionally. In short, the adop- tion fell through, the couple in despair stopped coming, and Nod renewed the old gaieties with Blinken, tossing off his disappointment in the following manner: "God is good, Blinken, and don't you forget it. God think to Himself like this: What shall I do with that child? Shall I send him to a man what can learn him the slide trombone? Or shall I keep him in the happy house? Now, the trombone is fine, but in the happy house Nod have a friend. So then God see that there is no choice nohow. 'Friendship come first,' God say."

Doberman didn't toss it off quite as spiritedly. He locked himself up in his office for three days and would admit no one but Belle, his secretary. She told me he just sat, for hours on end, his chin in his hands, muttering to himself occasionally, "A trombonist . . . imagine, a trombonist!"

One understands this. Music looks as if it might be a better world. On the fourth day he began to show his face again, the first of the many bizarre and mysterious attempts on his life occurred and he officially terminated the culture program. It hasn't been missed overmuch. The murder at- tempts have been a far richer source of amusement and have stimulated a great deal more discussion. I suppose there isn't much of a mystery here.

It was also at this time that Doberman began to neglect his personal cleanliness. He is trying to tell us something by it. One gets the message, of course, but what does he expect anybody to do about it?

One night around that time, he invited me out for a few beers. We sat in a bar in town, and he stared at his glass.

"Tough luck about Nod," I said.

"What? Oh yes . . . well, well, water under the bridge."

"Pincher really screwed the works, didn't he? You know, sir, if I were you—"

But he put a finger to his lips then. "Not another word, Bodkin. Poor Pincher . . . it wasn't entirely his fault. It is the result of a much larger catastrophe. I think in fact that everything here is much closer to being my fault than anyone else's."

"Don't be silly, sir."

"No, no, listen to me, Bodkin. Perhaps what is really needed here is another Lyle. He was the sort of director who was understood by everyone, and understood immediately! You smile—but I tell you, Bodkin, I am serious. And had I to do it over again, I would dye my skin black and make my first appearance here with a whip in one hand and a saber in the other. And I would enjoy it thoroughly. I'm becoming rather sick of myself, frankly."

Poor Doberman; all of a sudden one can't put up with it any more, one is driven under by it. I understood him when he said that what was needed here was a Lyle. Lyle was never driven under by this place. A superb administrator, he was always on top of it. He was Doberman's predecessor, a large black man who was here ten years, since the beginning. Then one day somebody offered him a larger salary elsewhere and he left.

He used to walk around in the courtyard for a bit in the morning with a leather strap, and let fly with it here and there as the fancy took him. He was indiscriminating too, was Lyle, and now and again used to get one of the staff as

well, across the calves or the side of the head. If you were
smart, you tried to stay out of his way, but it was impossible to guess when or where he would show up. He didn't
come only to the yard; he was cunning, like a child, and
was fond of taking you by surprise. It was hard to put up a
reasonable protest because surely you had done something,
or were thinking about doing something, for which that
stroke was nothing if not justice tempered with extreme
mercy. We all worshiped and cursed and laughed at him in
one breath, and he ruled like a passion. Occasionally he
would leave for a few days on a trip, and then the counselors drank some on the job, lay on the floors, sprawled in
the stairwells, laughed and danced in the courtyard and let
the inmates run amok for everybody's entertainment. It was
a holiday. From which fact one may draw whatever in-
ference one likes.

Doberman then, when he first stepped into office, found
himself in a holiday atmosphere. His first two hours he
spent up in the office; then at ten o'clock he came down into
the yard to have a look about. The inmates were running
around gayly, and the staff were running after, with their
belts in their hands, whipping anything they could get on to.
Three tables had been turned over at breakfast in the mess
hall. Knives and forks had been stolen and most of the
sharp instruments were gone from the infirmary.

The inmates thought it was a holiday again, you see. Lyle
was gone, and they couldn't quite make out what was
wrong with the counselors. It was a holiday. Why weren't
they acting like it was a holiday, and why the belts all of a
sudden? "The new director, man? He is a white faggit, anybody can see that. We going to have a holiday forever
now." But the staff weren't so sure. He hadn't spoken to any

of them yet, and until he did they'd play it safe. Lyle had
abandoned them, but he left behind his method and all that
day they hung on to it. They beat the inmates in the yard
and the passages, and winked among themselves in the mess
hall, where the proof of how many aches and pains they
had put into effect was demonstrated in the table manners
of their victims. As a result, most of the children ate the
afternoon and the evening meals with as fine a show of
delicacy as can be found among diners of the most rare and
expensive tastes. The staff had a sense of accomplishment.
Dissent continued, but by sundown it was laid low and in
hand by the scruff of the neck.

Doberman had walked into a mess; he looked at it for
two minutes, promptly returned to his office, locked himself
in, and nobody saw him again till later that night. After the
inmates were put to sleep, he posted the cooks to watch the
quarters, and rounded up the rest of the staff in the gymnasium.

"No child in this institution is ever again to be struck or
abused physically in any way—be me, by you, by anyone!"
he told us, by way of introducing himself. "And that goes
for hands, feet, belts or anything else you people have become accustomed to exercising upon them. Now, is that
clear?" It was a considerable blow. Nobody spoke up. He
had the law behind him in this, and one couldn't make an
open protest. He was right. He was enlightened. It was
embarrassing. The staff knew at once that they would have
to evade him too, just as they'd had to evade his predecessor. For different reasons though.

Lyle they evaded because they were afraid of the strap,
and besides it put you in good stead with the boys in your
group if you could somehow prove to them that you'd do

everything you could to protect them from him; and this one did, just so long as they behaved. But his shadow loomed over the yard and everywhere else, and the mention of his name was a charm. We used it sparingly so that the magic wouldn't wear. Usually a slap across the back of the head or a twist of an ear lobe sufficed. And one could do it in the open. Lyle even applauded this. But the whippings were his exclusive office. They were infrequent and all the more terrible because they were. Life for the children was equally as wretched then as it is now, but it was simpler for the counselors. One knew where one stood, and stood there and evaded him.

But Doberman had to be evaded because he would have your job if he caught you with a belt in hand, and yet you had to keep it in hand because if you didn't your group would go wild and you'd be fired anyway for not being able to control them. Perhaps the first mistake the Days made was in not stating the case openly to Doberman and letting him see what was what. Instead, they took him with a grain of salt and went about getting around the situation as best they could. The few who came right out with it and beat the inmates in the yard under Doberman's window were canned on the spot. They set an example; he meant business, did Doberman.

Almost everybody here needs the job and is in straits. The pay is a calculated humiliation; it attracts nobody but the untrained, the misfit, people without credentials or degrees to get them onto anything better, a few knights-errant and compulsive backbreakers. The backbreaker is most at home here—the job was made for him, he is in paradise. As for the knights-errant, they are not to be written off, it is in them that hope for something amenable lies, but they are satirized by everyone in Ulser except Doberman, and they don't last long, a couple of months at most. They are far and few between, anyway. In large part, it is those of us who are not fit, for one reason or another, to come to grips with a prettier way of life that remain. Perhaps if we all had courage we would clear out and make way for a higher order. But where would we go? The staff too are children, after all. Doberman is the one grownup in the place, and he is hopelessly outnumbered. In fact, he is against us. Lyle was over us, but Doberman is against us. Even the knights-errant give him what for as a matter of course.

Likely Doberman gave everything a lot of thought that first day alone in his office and came to asking himself: Shall we whip them or shall we not whip them? But he should never have posed the question to himself like that. It led him to lay the ground rules too explicitly, so that everyone understood at once, by instinct, precisely what was what. From then on we would come to the weekly staff meeting and talk Doberman's language with fervor, with sincerity even, and then go outside again and talk a quite different language, because Doberman doesn't make sense once the meeting is adjourned. One has to knock heads together, and that is an indispensable grammar. Those who couldn't handle it were either fired, quit or tried to switch over to nights.

I should have stood up that first meeting. "Sir," I should have said, "you don't understand. Somebody here has to beat them. And if you don't do it, we will!" Then it would have been in the open and we could have talked it over.

Doberman began making excursions right after that first meeting, walking around to see what was what. He aimed to keep a steady eye on everybody. The staff developed considerable skill in the art of covering up their transgressions. There are certain safe corners, certain times of the day. In the second week he caught one of the counselors engaged in a vigorous tangle with a little boy who was having a tantrum with a baseball bat. The counselor had the boy by the throat and was punching him in the ribs. Doberman ordered the man to let go and began a reasonable and gentle discourse, but before he could get the second sentence under way the bat pushed his head against the wall and he was laid up in bed for a week. He returned to work armed with a new caution but essentially unchanged. He continues to talk to the children as though between him and them there were a common cause. In response, they are sullen and suspicious, or they try to get something out of him in the style of carnival confidence men, an extravagantly roguish style that appeals to Doberman's love of losing. Often he promises that he will see to their requests, and he does; he goes directly to the counselor and orders the thing done. The counselor then beats the child in the closet, and there it ends.

As the years pass, Doberman comes less and less frequently to the courtyard to talk to the boys, and the staff meetings grow longer and more ornate. There he is on firm ground, and everyone treats him with deference. For two hours a week he is king and doesn't bother us at all. If one accepts the sly mythology upon which everything he says is founded, then it's pretty. Everything follows. It is even a relief to think of the place in that way for a couple of hours a week, and one goes to the meetings with an expectation similar to that of going to the theater. His imagination is a gushing spring, he always has some new development, and anybody who in a fit of conscience attempts to break up the show is immediately looked upon as a bore and a killjoy by everyone.

Of course, it has been clear to Doberman for a long time what the staff are up to. He confides it all to me: he knows, he understands, he is infinite in his mercy, but he cannot walk in the yard without making an idiot of himself. He has even come to understand his position here—that he is an entertainer, that it's his duty to dazzle for two hours a week with fine talk, to lift the Days out of the mire for a bit, and that's that. He lives for those two hours, poor Doberman, and spends a lot of time preparing his lectures.

Oddly enough, his lectures are not so far out of good sense as one might imagine. The reason his enlightened program won't work here is quite simple: the geography of the place isn't set up for it. We're too crowded. One hundred and eighty outlaws have been lifted out of an urban wreckage and jammed together like an army. Against this army there is a single neurotic Irish psychiatrist from the Midwest, who visits once a week in the afternoon. And he is quite alone, is Dr. Sweeney, because as he himself has said, "The day shift are scarcely distinguishable from the inmates."

Doberman's previous job, at which he had worked fifteen years, was presiding over a quite different kind of children. He invited me over to his house one night about five years ago and showed me a silent movie that he made of them. It was jumpy and amateurish enough, but I got the idea. He lives alone, poor Doberman, and was feeling dimly nostalgic that night. He wanted me to get a glimpse of what his life was like before Ulser. So I sat and watched while he explained a few things, but mainly he too stared at the screen. I have a flat and sinister notion of those children because it was through Doberman's dime-store projector that I saw them. Dreamy little angels, they seem to me. They never grow up. They cannot control their organs or their muscles; their tongues flop out of their mouths blithely. Their heads bob like corks in water and favor one shoulder. Their curiosity, which is figured in their wide eyes, is perpetual and insatiable because their intellects are incapable of feeding it much. When death comes, whatever the pain, it appears to them to be no more curious and inexplicable than anything else. Or maybe it does. They have more than their share of pimples; their bodies are lopsided; the heads are too big, the faces puffy. On the whole they must be fairly easy to handle, and they seem to get along well enough with their peers; they simply stare at one another in wonder and delight. Their teachers, dedicated and well trained, lavish affection and a strict, hard, American optimism on them year after year, in hopes that they may learn at least the alphabet and the beginning of the multiplication table before death comes waltzing in—so that when they go to meet their Maker, they will be able to recite a few austerities for Him.

This then is where Doberman came from: a world of children for whom life was one long series of miracles from beginning to end. "In short, Bodkin," he concluded after showing me the film, "I have come to Ulser from what now looks like paradise, and am having a bit of difficulty in getting used to the idea still."

One of Doberman's favorite topics in staff meetings is the "suburban, the *in*tegrated foster home, gentlemen." He will go on at great length, though he knows that none of us can do anything about it. He seems to take pleasure in simply enlightening us. But at the bottom of his quiet talk about

foster homes is a loud dream, the dream of a dispersion.
What he would like to do is lock all American Negro children into that "paradise" of his and teach them how to bob
their heads before the miracles of life. "Otherwise there is
no hope, Bodkin. The ghetto grows, and then you have a
monster on your hands. The dignity of a passionate race
has to go or you'll never put a stop to their monkey business."

I understand this. It's been done before, dispersion has,
with considerable success. Doberman understands it too.
He used to love to use the Jews as a case in point—only in
private with me though. He sees a remarkable similarity
between us and the Negroes, and carries the comparison a
bit far, beyond good taste even; he has never shown very
fine manners on this subject. "Governments," he will say,
"have always understood you Jews all too well, Bodkin.
They scattered you about and put up walls about your tents
with good reason. Given freedom to propagate and to develop your natural inclinations, you'd have brought a jeal-
ous wrath on this earth, a holocaust and a blood bath that
would have made Hitler himself look like a schoolgirl by
comparison. The suffering of the Jews has been a stroke of
luck. Perhaps it may teach you to dance again. You think I
am talking through my hat? That I am speaking in bad
taste? Bodkin, listen to me. I am not one of your irrespon-
sible monsters. I have given these matters some thought, my
son. Why, just look at your literature! It is only Job and
Isaiah that are ever spoken of by your elegant clean-shaven
Jews nowadays in public. But the rest? The rest is hidden
away behind curtains like an embarrassment. It all smacks
too much of bureaucratic confusion and the righteousness
of a foolish people, of the intolerably magnanimous men of
old. Oh, when your wonderful Messiah comes, of course,

then you will bring all your precious old books out into the open again; but until then, silence. None of you dare speak of anything but the misery of the age, and the horror that is upon your fellow-men, even gentiles."

Doberman has large notions. His mind moves over the whole earth and therefore is incapable of governing poor little Ulser effectively. He has no sense of the peculiar logic of the place. He is perpetually adrift. His mind can focus on a single human being, or over an entire race at once, but on nothing in between. In fact, he belongs on the night shift with the rest of us. Or the university, where he could dazzle with a literate discontent. He might even make a successful novelist, because his point of view—except for his medieval opinion of the Jews—would appeal to a reader of taste. I can see him now, marching pen in hand, with an unflagging will to creation, under the flag of despair. It makes a happy combination, and he could go far.

I really like the man in a way, and he likes me as well. We understand one another. It is not in him to be other than he is. He is the butt of ridicule, but that has never proved anything.

It's too bad he never remarried. A helpmate is what he needs. He sits home alone most nights and looks at his face wrinkling up over the window pane. Or he reads. He reads "history." Poets he won't have—prose is what he is after. But it does him no good. His head is crammed full of the bone pile, of the muck and malice of all the generations of vipers in print, and it has played him in the long run a dirty trick, has history, whipped him into the impotent fervor of the pious and strangled his faith. He hasn't a pot or a window to throw it out of. He is a widower. Two months after he took his doctorate from Princeton he married a Negro girl. This was about twenty-five years ago, at a time in this country when there were no circles to speak of in which such a marriage was fashionable and very few in which it was acceptable. He showed me a picture of her once—a homely thin slip of a woman. She was nineteen years old at her wedding. She was the only child of a poor family. Her father was a choleric man with intellectual yearnings and a third-grade education. He read voraciously and shined shoes in a barbershop till the day he died. The night that Doberman returned from his elopement to announce himself as a son-in-law, the old man slapped his face and threw him and his bride out bodily. He was patriarchal, this old man. He despised whites, he despised Negroes, he despised Doberman and he despised shoes. It is said that he worked barefoot, gave the most spitefully elegant spit shine on the West Side, and was capable of holding forth with more passionate and crisp eloquence on the exigencies of political murder than any man since Richard the Third. He was not handsome, had a game leg and died of his own gall, quietly, in bed. He died just a few months after his daughter. After two years of married life she threw herself out a window, and Doberman says, "It was my fault, Bodkin," which doesn't do anybody any good, but he is fond of saying it. Has grown increasingly fond, in fact, every year since. Suddenly, out of nowhere, he will shake his head and mumble, "It is my fault—all . . . all my fault." At first, I thought that perhaps he was saying this in response to the painful memory of his young wife. But now I am wiser and understand that it's not that at all—that the cause of this inappropriate remark is unknown to him. "It is all . . . all my fault." An incalculable burden, to be sure. Once when he made this remark during a discussion on the rising cost of living, I replied promptly that it certainly was his fault, and "Just how do you propose to make amends, sir?" I smiled, but he was puzzled; he had not heard himself. This was my first important insight into his character. "It is all my fault" is always said by him absently. It is simply a bad habit.

In spite of everything, however, he is to be commended: for six consecutive years he has managed to keep a straight face in the midst of an institutional hilarity. For a man like Doberman this is no mean achievement.

Or at least he managed to keep a straight face until two months ago. At this point I think there is cause to be concerned over what may be going on in that haunted mind of his.

That Nod believes him to be the murderer of Page is also a matter of some concern. It's even creepy. I don't like the idea that anyone should entertain such a thought. He's a strange little boy, is Nod. *"Do you think I done it?" "Did what?" "Kill Page."* Where does he get such ideas? On the one hand he believes that Doberman killed Page; on the other he believes that people suspect *him* of having killed Page.

There he goes now, on the second landing of the fire escape. He raises the window and slips in, then pops his head out and waves the paper sack with his dirty socks in it at me. I wave back. Everything is in order.

I make my way across the field and around toward the front of the building. I am late for the meeting.

"Just don't tell nobody I was running, okay? My counselor, he will beat me something terrible for it if he finds out. Please?"

There was no cleverness in that appeal, none at all. It addressed itself too exclusively to the good, and he will never get along in this world if he persists in going about his affairs in such a fashion.

ACCUSED AND
DEFENDED

Miss Rose stares out over the courtyard from her room on the second story; a yellow light glows at her back. She pulls up the window and calls out, "Who is it?"

"It's me—Bodkin. Why aren't you at the meeting, Miss Rose?"

"I'm waiting, waiting, my boy. For the findings of the autopsy. What do I care for meetings, eh?"

She closes the window, and I go on up to Doberman's office. He informs me, by way of salutation, that I'm a half-hour late. It's a solemn caucus: the watchmen, Doberman, Pincher, Libby, Dew and Peduza.

Boober alone is not solemn. He is melancholy, as ever, a rock in the current. He looks straight ahead. His tears—how was it that Ashe put it to me once? "His tears, like an old tradition, flow out of a source that one can name but not satisfactorily discover." I look into Boober's eyes as into a well in which I can't see my reflection. Rumor has it that he has to wring out his pillow over the bathtub when he wakes, and that he keeps three on hand because it requires two days for each to dry after he has slept on it. If sleep won't put an end to his lamentations, one wonders if the grave will either. It will be a curious eternity for him.

He's been drinking; they all have. He, Weasel, Trembley and Ashe—the room stinks like a brewery. The four of them have one of their bouts at least once a month. I used to go along, but have given it up the past couple years. It is too exacting an enterprise, my constitution isn't up to it, and even the best brew is not the best diversion in the sedentary life of a valetudinarian like me. I prefer to swing on the parallels at the gym, and when the weather permits, to dig the garden I've been allowed behind the staff house. Save Trembley, who takes in liquor as unremittingly as Boober exudes tears, they all have a tough time recuperating.

"You are a half-hour late, Bodkin," says Doberman, thinking, I suppose, that I didn't hear him the first time.

"Where's Miss Rose?" I say.

"She is not here," he says autocratically.

"Yes, I noticed. Too bad though. We could use her."

"Use?"

"To liven things up."

I look for a chair in the circle, but Doberman clears his throat. "Where have you been, Bodkin?" he says.

"Been?"

"You seem to be making a habit of tardiness. And this time, if I may say so, it is like a smack in the face."

"I overslept."

"Haven't you an alarm clock?"

"I don't like them."

"There are many things, Mr. Bodkin, which we do not like, but which, because of their utility, we must endure nevertheless."

This is not like Doberman at all. Look at him. He has taken a bath and doused himself with cologne; I can smell it across the room. He wears a wide blue tie painted with extravagant blossoms, a pin-stripe suit, a forest-green vest and shoes pointed at the toe. He has had a manicure too and has raked his forelock loose across the right temple. There is no question but that he means business and has come at last down to earth from that shady cloud of his. I am less reassured by this than touched; I smile.

"Sit down, son," he says.

"Okay."

"Now, where have you been?"

"I told you, sir. I overslept."

"Extraordinary."

"I don't see why."

"Because I called the staff house at a quarter to nine, and Handy said that you had just rushed out the door, with a sandwich in your hand."

"I was overcome by the cold along the way and fell asleep in the woods."

"I don't think this is a time for cleverness, Bodkin."

"I'm not being clever."

"I'm glad you understand that fact. I was afraid you thought you were."

"Not at all. That's just the way it happened. I was walking along, sir, with every intention of getting here on time, and then, you know, I got winded all of a sudden, and thought I'd sit down on a rock and have a smoke. I leaned back against a tree, I looked up at the sky, and the next thing I know I'm in wonderland, I'm dreaming."

"What did you dream about?"

"I forget."

"In the future you ought to try to recall your dreams. They may provide you with some insight into yourself."

"There's not much there to see into, I'm afraid, sir. Thanks just the same."

"Dear sweet Bodkin," says Boober to himself.

"What have I missed so far?" I say.

"Very little," says Doberman. "We have been waiting for you. Mr. Pincher spoke a little on . . . on Dr. Sweeney's innovation in bedsheets." He looks away from me uneasily and adds, "Among other things."

Pincher gives me a crooked smile.

"And where is the doctor?" I say.

"Dr. Sweeney could not be reached," says Pincher, glad of the opportunity to assert himself, to be informative and to pronounce the great doctor's name. "But he will be here the day after tomorrow as usual."

"What about Miss Rose?" I say. If I persist in asking about her, maybe I can get Pincher's goat a little.

"We thought it best—" he begins.

But Doberman interrupts. "She is tired," he says. "Now, if I may, I should like to get to the business at hand."

Miss Peduza begins to cry, and Doberman, annoyed, glances at her. "Last night a child died—" he begins, and she tries to stifle the noise in her handkerchief.

"And I think that it is not unfair to say," he continues, "that each of us here in this room ought to feel responsible, at least in part, for this tragedy. While the responsibility, of course, cannot be divided among us alone, it is my personal feeling that it does, nevertheless, fall more directly upon us than upon anyone else, and ought to be acknowledged accordingly." He narrows his eyes and looks us over, with a subtle fear and uncertainty that makes one distrust every word.

He crosses his legs. "The acknowledgement of a responsibility for a tragedy which is beyond recall, however, is often a simple exercise in silliness, in that it may lead one to a debilitating despair—which, in certain circles, I've been told, is indeed considered a wonderful achievement. Now, I think that everyone at some time or another should make the acquaintance of despair, else he may be intolerable to his less fortunate neighbors and will have a difficult time in learning compassion. However, since all of you are sufficiently desperate people, I think it unnecessary to lecture you further into the abyss. But I shall lecture you. Because . . . because I'm your director, you see, and I've put on a new suit for the occasion.

"I have just stated that the responsibility was divided among us. Don't misunderstand. To divide responsibility is to divide a packet of seeds. The whole packet is very light, but one seed planted in each of you grows into a heavy contemplative creature. If, on the one hand, it contemplates exclusively the graves of injustice, the creature will grow inward, as though by taking that malignant turn, it should somehow reach into the past itself and destroy the injustice therein; whereas in fact it reaches into nothing but one's own frailties, and accomplishes the destruction not of any injustice, but simply of one's own life and whatever possibilities it may contain. If, on the other hand, this creature of ours contemplates rather what is yet to come, it will take root in that which has passed, and grow outward—"

"I find it amazing, sir," interrupts Libby, "that you feel it necessary to lecture us in this fashion. What you have to say is merely a matter of certain simplicities, which we all of us have heard a thousand times. 'Don't eat yourself up inside.' Isn't that what it boils down to?"

"I'm not sure what it boils down to, Mr. Libby." Doberman flushes; veins appear on his forehead. "And I am not even sure whether or not it boils. However, I apologize if I have been amazing you for a few moments with simplicities, for that was not my intention. Apparently you are very easily amazed. I think no one else in this room has been amazed. Is anyone else amazed?"

Libby looks at each of us in hopes he will find someone willing to speak up. The poor fellow needs support, and I am almost tempted to give it to him.

"I suppose no one else is amazed," he says.

"I suppose not," says Doberman.

"What about you, Mr. Dew? Aren't you amazed?"

Mr. Dew, black as he is, blushes and looks at the floor. He is a big man with a long powerful neck that curves outward at the back, as though a straight one were insufficient to pillar his pride. He never removes his big felt hat and is invariably dressed in an undershirt and an old tweed jacket. He sits between his two white partners, Libby and Peduza; it is obvious that he pities them.

"And what about you, Mr. Boober?" says Libby, nervously excited. "Trembley? Ashe? Anyone? Ah well, you're right. Nobody is amazed. Not even Mr. Bodkin. But he is habitually late, so that we can't be sure. He may come around."

"If I may interrupt," says Doberman, "I should like to point out to you that it was principally for the benefit of Mr. Bodkin that I spoke as I did. He is one of those, to borrow a phrase, who eats himself up inside."

"That's debatable."

"But this, you see, this is not a debate, Mr. Libby. You don't seem to understand that."

"I understand it all too well. I've been here six months, haven't I? By now I have the order of the day. We sit around and nod at one another; then we leave the room and take up the same old atrocities. The point is, sir, that the method of your discourse is very pretty indeed, but frankly, in the end one is hard put to find its pertinence."

"Is that a fact?"

"A hard fact, yes."

"Perhaps then you have a more pertinent method."

"Perhaps I do."

"By all means then, Mr. Libby, let's have it."

"All right, you'll have it."

"Good then, good!"

"And when I'm done, you can fire me if you like—"

"Now, now, Mr. Libby—"

"That's right! I don't need this job, you see, and that pittance you call a pay check. I have a master's degree, excellent references—in physics!—and can get five times the money I get here, and ten times the satisfaction. Unlike the rest of you, I'm here because I want to be, not because I have to be."

Poor Libby checks himself, abashed at his own words.

He knows he has taken the wrong tack and is painfully aware that he doesn't understand the amenities.

"Go ahead, Mr. Libby," says Doberman, visibly gathering poise out of Libby's discomfort. "We are listening."

Libby fumbles for a cigarette, stands up, returns the pack to his pocket without having taken a cigarette out, reaches for the pack again, evidently decides that it will make him look too foolish, and forgoes the pleasure.

I had a dream the other day about Libby and his boys. Mr. Dew and Miss Peduza were in it too. It all took place on a ship. Libby and Peduza are on deck; I am watching from the bridge. The boys of Group Three scramble up from out of the hatches. Miss Peduza assails them in a foreign tongue. They sulk; she persists. They attack her in a body; Mr. Libby admonishes. This cheers their effort; they beat her. She is not pretty; she has too many teeth. She cannot speak English tolerably and so is unable to reason with them. Libby, however, reasons with them. But they are not reasonable. The ship groans. Mr. Dew shinnies down the mast from the crow's-nest. He whips off his belt and lashes the air. The boys quiet. They kneel and weep. Miss Peduza composes herself. She runs to Mr. Dew, cries on his shoulder and thanks him. The little children thank him too. He orders them into single file and straps them soundly, and they thank him for that as well. To all save Libby it is a gracious occasion. He leans over the rail and listens to reason.

It was an accurate dream as far as it went. Dew is the whip master of the group, but Libby deplores violence and terror and won't lay a hand on the inmates. He and Dew have frequent arguments about method in front of the boys. The boys take advantage of this and play them against each other quite effectively. Miss Peduza is an oddity; why she is here I don't know. She is a Latin American, extremely unhappy at her job, and lonely. The group is a large mess. The other fourteen groups are under control; each of them is ruled by three counselors who agree on the method of approach. Like Mr. Dew, most of them have a natural talent for terrorism, coupled with a genuine concern for the well-being of their boys, and are graceful with the belt.

Libby is thin and pale with a clear skin and very clean teeth. He affects dungarees and a lumber jacket. He is pleasant to look at except that his right eye has a slight twitch, which is at present extremely active. Beads of sweat appear on his brow; he has worked himself up into a highly nervous state.

"You talk about *seeds,* a packet of *seeds,*" he says sarcastically to Doberman. "That's fine, fine. Well and good! The plain truth of the matter is that nearly the entire packet for this particular misfortune belongs to Mr. Bodkin alone."

"A moment, sir!" cries Ashe.

"Let him finish," says Doberman.

"This 'Dear sweet Bodkin' of yours," says Libby, his mouth twisted with disdain, "who allegedly eats himself up inside, is—according to my impression of him, which is based on only a few but very lengthy conversations—he is in fact no more nor less than a pretentious little snob, who has unsystematically read himself into an extravagant confusion and indulges himself night and day in the perusal of his own lack of conviction. It is, to be sure, a humble enough indulgence, and I certainly wouldn't send him to hell for it. But he has raised it to such a pitch, has made such a fetish of it, that he very nearly provides us with an embodiment in his own person of that . . . what?—that which is bringing this institution so quickly to its collapse. Now, I haven't examined Mr. Bodkin's mind; neither am I qualified to, nor would I care to if I were. I allude only to the fact which was pointed out to us by you, Mr. Pincher, before Mr. Bodkin arrived."

"Fact?" cries Ashe. "Fact? Fact?"

Libby ignores him and looks directly at me. "The tapes of your time clock, Mr. Bodkin, are completely blank for the past three years. The tapes of the previous years have apparently been destroyed. According to Mr. Pincher's calculations, there ought to have been in the neighborhood of sixteen thousand marks for the three-year period, each one of them a symbol of your having made your appointed round on the half-hour. It is entirely possible, of course, that the symbol of your performance is not correspondent with the performance itself. I am not a one to judge a man by the marks on a tape. Therefore let me ask you man to man, point blank: is that tape a fairly accurate indication of the manner in which you have performed your duties over the past three years, or is it not?"

"Do you *hear*, Mr. Doberman?" says Ashe, fairly choking with indignation. "This silly young man ... is very close to accusing Bodkin of—'This is an outrage, sir. I demand you stop it at once."

"There is quite enough demanding at present, Mr. Ashe," says Doberman out of the side of his mouth as he lights his pipe and watches the flame with an Olympian air. "Let Mr. Bodkin answer the question."

"Well, Bodkin?" says Libby. "Is it, or isn't it?"

"Yes," I say, "it's an accurate indication."

"Bodkin," says Boober, in a gentle, paternal way, "what are you saying? These tapes of theirs are not an accurate indication of anything, not even of themselves."

"Boober is right," says Ashe. "Defend yourself, Bodkin, and let this poor lost sheep hear the voice that we have heard."

"But he's got a point there, Ashe—a very good point," I say.

"No more of that, lad," says Trembley, screwing up his face at me. "Where's your spirit, eh? Can't you see this Libby fellow here doesn't care a bit for what's what, that he's just spoiling for a fight and testing out his muscles on you? And you sit there and tell him he's got a *point*— it's a shameful condition. Let him have what for, lad. Be a man."

Libby delivers me a scornful smile. "You heard them, Mr. Bodkin. They want you to defend yourself. What do you have to say? Nothing? I thought so. That's quite typical, isn't it. You're remarkably consistent. But let me enlighten you further. The tapes of the other watchmen were also investigated by Mr. Pincher—and what d'you think? The tapes of Trembley, Ashe and Boober show that while they were not so conscientious as to have punched in the full sixteen thousand times, they nevertheless had done so several thousand apiece. Which indicates, at least to me, that they have a certain moderate interest in and respect for the necessary banalities."

They hang their heads, my three buddies, and won't look me in the eye. I think they feel that they have betrayed me in some way and are ashamed. They must think that I believe they punched their clocks out of malice to me. But that is foolish. I couldn't be more pleased; why should they feel guilty for having displayed good sense and done their duty?

"As for Mr. Weasel," says Libby, "he has exceeded the limits of duty, and shows *sev*enteen thousand and some odd marks. Here, at least, we have in one man an admirable, sociable mentality in which there is a basis for hope. I have merely to think of Mr. Weasel in order to assure myself that all is not lost."

"I don't like it," mutters Weasel, looking at the floor. He is bent forward with his forearms resting on his knees.

"What, Mr. Weasel?" says Libby.

"I say I don't like it."

"What is it you don't like?"

"The way you point that skinny finger of yours."

"There you have, gentlemen, a fighting spirit." Libby addresses the group at large, forces himself to smile proudly and points his finger at Weasel.

Weasel looks up at him from under lowered brows. "I say I don't like you pointing."

"But I am not pointing a finger of accusation, Mr. Weasel, I—"

"I don't care what you pointing, man. I say I don't like you point, period. If you want to point, point yourself. Because next time you point me, you are like to get your pointer bit off."

"Good for you, Weasel," says Ashe happily.

"Shut off, nigger," says Weasel. "Lest I give you a good-for-you you never forget. Mr. Doberman, can't you please take this meet in hand? We're wasting time here over nothing."

"In a moment," says Doberman. "I believe Mr. Libby has still a few more opinions to get off his chest. Let's hear him out, and then we shall proceed. Mr. Libby?"

"You're right," says Libby. "I do. I knew that my remarks would meet with hostility of this sort, and I was prepared for it. It is simply that no one has ever spoken frankly at this institution, and when suddenly someone has the courage to do so, the effect at first is bound to be one of shock—"

"Get to the point, Mr. Libby."

"But the point, you see, has already been made, sir, by Mr. Bodkin himself just a moment ago. He demonstrated before everyone in this room, and to the avowed disappointment of his co-workers, that he is a defeated man, that he not only accepts defeat but accepts it with open arms, and takes a kind of pleasure in it that would seem to be very perverse indeed. Any man who is unwilling to take up the defense of his own dignity can scarcely be expected to defend the dignity of others. Now, I don't say that there is no room for his type in this world; I say only that he has been engaged for the past nine years in a trade for which he is eminently unsuitable. I should think he'd make an excellent librarian or a garbage collector. But here, decidedly, his resignation, disinterest and quietude are a palpable menace which leads, as we all witnessed yesterday, to the death of innocent children. Not a single mark on the tape! D'you see what that means, Bodkin? That's not mere laziness and lack of interest. That's a banner—a zealous allegiance to futility itself. And then, on top of it, as if you'd felt you hadn't made your position clear enough, you made sure to arrive a half-hour late to the meeting whose very purpose was to discuss the tragedy of which your lateness was the direct cause. Mr. Doberman said your coming late was like 'a smack in the face.' I think the metaphor merciful and mild. He waited for you three hours last night, didn't he, and a half-hour tonight. How long is this to go on? Do you understand, Bodkin, that had you been making your bed checks on the half-hour, as you agreed in your contract to do, you might have prevented the death of an innocent child? No, I don't think you do understand. So for your own and the institution's good, I recommend either that you quit your job or that you be dismissed forthwith. As for me, I refuse to work another day in the same organization with a murderer—"

"What?" cries Ashe. "Bodkin? A murderer?"

"Yes, that's right," says Libby, with composure, to Ashe, and then turns to me and shakes his finger with vehemence. "And I'll leave if you don't—d'you hear? And I will write letters, I promise you, to every reputable newspaper in the state and expose you and the institution and all the evils it entertains!" He pauses, looks at me for a moment as if I had just insulted him, and then sits down. "I've had my say. Thank you."

"Thank you, Mr. Libby," says Doberman, smiling strangely at me.

Libby's frankness hangs in the air like the blade of a guillotine; I would like to say something casual, anything, to set him and the others at ease.

Miss Peduza turns to Mr. Dew and says, "What say Mr. Libby, please?"

To which he replies, "Him say Mr. Bodkin kill Page."

Though I've told Dew a thousand times that it is ridiculous for him to speak with her in that style, and that if he would talk to her simply, slowly and correctly, she would soon learn a proper English, he persists, and so continues to be the only one she seems to understand.

"Mr. Bodkin kill Page?" she says, amazed. "Is true?"

"Me not know," he says. "Ask Mr. Bodkin."

"Mr. Bodkin," she says, "is true? You kill Page?"

"No, Miss Peduza," I say.

"No?"

"No."

"Did you hear that, Mr. Libby?" says Ashe, rising up joyfully. "He said, 'No.' Bodkin said, 'No.' Good for you, Bodkin. Hallelujah, sir!" He beams at the entire company, spreads out his hands, brings them back to his lapels, sits down, and turning a strict face to Libby, says, "Bodkin is capable, sir, of a direct and dignified answer. Not always, of course—only when the question is also direct and dignified. Your questions were such a tangle, however, that our Bodkin was at a pass. You left him but two choices: to be silent or abusive. And therefore, for a man of his character, no choice at all."

"Excuse me," says Libby. "I'd like to say—"

"Excuse *me*, sir!" cries Ashe. "Excuse *me!*" He fairly leaps out of his chair, across the room to Miss Peduza's side, and caresses her shoulder. "Consider now this young lady. What little talent she has with the language, she has turned to good account; that is to say, she has got herself another talent with it: the talent, sir, for asking *plain questions*. But what, may I ask, have *you* done with *your* talent for the language? I shall tell you. You have buried it, alas, under a heap of complications. Just so. Let us understand, sir, that the fact of Bodkin's being *close* to little Page does not indicate that Bodkin was the *death* of little Page. Listen a moment to a skeleton of your speech." He ticks off each point on his pinky. "Bodkin does not punch clocks. Not punching clocks murders little boys. Therefore? Bodkin is a murderer." He makes his eyes big and round, cocks his head to one side and lowers his voice. "And so happily do your sentences run on that at first, I confess, one is tempted to run after. Yes indeed. May God forgive the both of us!"

He crosses himself elaborately, walks slowly through his captive audience back to his chair, and sitting down with considerable majesty, "Ah, my dear Mr. Libby," he says, "you, of all the people in this room, as both a Christian and a scientist, ought to know better. But you don't. Unlike Bodkin—who is a mere Jew and a bookworm—unlike Bodkin, you do not understand, you do not consider. It would seem that you are far less a man engaged in the pursuit of knowledge than a sad victim still of some very old habits. Many is the time"—here Ashe sighs heavily— "many is the time that I, unnoticed, have passed Mr. Bodkin's sitting room . . . and do you know what I see there? I see Mr. Bodkin sitting, sir. Correct. I see him with a book. I see him engaged, in short, in the glory of literature. And do you know what I think in those moments? I think: Read, my dear Bodkin Because I have a fear. I have a fear that if ever you should give it up, the walls of Ulser would crumble! Do you see, sir? You have said that it is Bodkin who will bring the walls down, but I say that it is he who has been keeping them up. How? I shall tell you . . ."

Suddenly he is at the window, his ear close to the pane, his eyes darting to each of us in turn in a desperate attempt to translate his wonderful fear. "There are vast armies of words, sir, assembling at the gates—did you know? Yes! Listen . . . do you hear? Well? Who will defend us from the onslaught? Most of us, as Mr. Boober so often has said, are 'preoccupied.' Mr. Boober himself weeps, I am given to prayer, Mr. Trembley tipples and Mr. Weasel, alas, has his little iniquities. Who then is there among us clock punchers to do battle nightly with the word? Eh? Bodkin alone. He, sir, reads. He sits in his chair and reads. And though you think his reading to no purpose, and words mere creatures of the fancy, you are mistaken. Because the pen is mightier than the sword, sir, and it is the reader who takes the wound. For all of us!"

He leaves the window, head down, hands clasped behind his back, and paces around the outside of the circle so that we all have to turn our necks this way and that to follow him. "I know what you will say to this; you will say, 'I don't see the relevance.' You will say that I have made a high and general apology for a low misdemeanor. But let us consider. It is true that Bodkin has violated a contract. Nine years ago he agreed to inspect thirty-six beds on the half-hour, every working night. And he has not done so. But why should he? What would he see there but sleepers? If ever there were a child awake, there would be a sound, and every little whisper, even the drop of a pin, in this resonant edifice, may be heard from his chair in the sitting room. Had Page cried out, had he made but the feeblest sign, Bodkin would, under ordinary conditions, have known."

"Well then?" says Pincher, impatiently. "Why didn't he know?"

Ashe stops walking. He leans backward, drawing his chin into his throat, and raises his eyebrows at Pincher. "For one thing, *you,* Mr. Pincher, came uninvited to keep him from his books. And for another, your immodest voice, sir, so filled the halls hour upon hour that *were* there some little cry of pain, no one, not *anyone,* would have heard."

"Mr. Ashe," begins Pincher.

"And after *you,*" Ashe interrupts, "we clock punchers likewise came to keep him from his books, and filled the halls with *our* voices. And then came Miss Rose, God bless

[101]

her, and her voice is not small either. And Bodkin was the one who took care of her, I might add, escorting her to her apartment off and on again the whole night through. Miss Rose takes care of the sick, sir, but Bodkin takes care of Miss Rose—"

"Before you go any further, let us understand," says Pincher, very much annoyed, "that I had come to see Mr. Bodkin with an important message. In regards certain innovations—"

"Ah yes!" says Ashe, raising one finger in the air. "Innovations—in spies and *bed*sheets—and these innovations *too* made a noise. You see, it is a wonder that Bodkin was able even to hear himself think. As to conscientiousness, I must also inform everyone that when the footsteps of the tramp were heard in our halls last night, it was Bodkin, sir, who took the initiative to investigate. In short, Mr. Libby," he proclaims, drawing himself up to his full height, his grayish brown-and-purple face looming over us now like a thundercloud, "the only thing that I find at all amazing, sir, in this discussion tonight is the accusation you have brought against Mr. Bodkin."

"Who is perfect, I suppose," says Libby, a bored expression on his youthful face.

"No sir, not perfect," replies Ashe. "He has a fault. He is a Jew. But the Lord, I assure you, in His infinite mercy will forgive him that."

"You mean you consider that a *fault?*" says Libby. He makes a great show of being shocked by this and amused.

"The Jews killed Christ, sir. It is written," says Ashe with solemnity. "But Bodkin did not kill Page. Not Page. This you may take as absolute. I am in daily communication with the angels, sir, and they are singing to me, this very moment, of his innocence . . . You are smiling, Mr. Libby. Why do you smile? The angels, sir! This is not a laughing matter."

My defender stands staring with a defiant faith at Libby. In response, Libby smiles unpleasantly.

The others are embarrassed—for me, probably because they suppose Ashe has disqualified his argument by showing that he is a lunatic. Which he may well be—not, as may be supposed, because he communicates with angels or believes that one killed Christ, but because he has attempted to defend an indefensible Bodkin like myself. Boober, elbows on knees, puts his head in his hands and shakes it from side to side, muttering at the floor.

AUTOPSY

D on't you see, Mr. Ashe," says Libby, "that there are no such things as 'ordinary conditions' in a place like this? It is for the very reason that the night often is not, in fact, as quiet as Mr. Bodkin would like it to be, that it's absolutely imperative Mr. Bodkin abide by his contract and make his rounds on the half-hour, that he shine his flashlight into every bed periodically, that he not wait for danger to show itself but go look for it—"

Voices are raised outside and the outer door crashes. Handy and Miss Rose are shouting in the vestibule. The office door opens a crack and then is slammed shut. It opens and slams again, then again.

Pincher leaps to his feet and throws open the door. Miss Rose, our lady of the flowers, is slapping Hanover Jones, who, it seems, has been destined to encounter more acerbity in doorways than a house-to-house salesman. He has an envelope in his right hand, which he keeps extended behind him well out of her reach, so that only his left is free to ward her off. Pincher steps between them and gets a clout in the process, while Handy takes advantage of the intervention to slip out of the fray, into the circle of reason, and drop the envelope in Doberman's lap.

"Give it to me!" cries Miss Rose. "It's mine, mine!"

She struggles in Pincher's arms, but he is too big for her.

"Now, now," he says.

"That is a medical communication, Mr. Doberman," she says.

"I am well aware—" begins Doberman.

"Aware! You're aware of nothing. Well, well, look at you now! All spiffed up! It's about time, I'd say."

"Never mind, Miss Rose." Doberman blushes.

"I hope you've had a change of underclothes as well. For the past two months you've been a bacterial menace, I don't mind telling you— Ah God, never mind indeed. Give it to me at once, sir. Your authority ends where mine and medicine begins. Besides, it's likely to be in Latin."

"Latin, Miss Rose?"

"That Frankenstein!" she says. "The pathologist! D'you know him? The man in the morgue! Yes, Latin. He has gone in for Latin in his dotage. Let me—let me go, Pincher! Idiot!"

Doberman says gently, "Let her go, Mr. Pincher."

He does. She shakes herself straight, catches her breath

and flies at Doberman and the envelope. But Pincher is on
the spot; he hauls her off and plants her in a chair, where
she folds up and goes to pieces.

"How shamelessly I'm treated!" she wails, the tears
streaming down her face. "Isn't it mine, the message?"

"Why, of *course*, Miss Rose," says Doberman. "But—"

"I know you, Mr. Doberman, how fond you are of putting a veil of secrecy over every statement of fact. I simply
can't . . . you must have pity on me—I simply can't put up
with another such. Not in this case. Please, for my own
peace of mind, I beg you, let us have this one plain. I'm an
old woman, such an old woman. One atom of reasonableness is all I ask of this life before it gives me over. I understand the language of the pathologist, do you see? It is a
precise language. The words have a destination. They run
on after good sense. To the tutored eye, believe me, it's a
very pretty sight. Let me, please . . . my whole life, don't
you see?"

Doberman tears open the envelope and takes out the
letter. "You were right. It is in Latin, Miss Rose. How
curious—"

"See? Didn't I tell you?" she says excitedly. "Here, I beg
you, give it over. I'll translate for you."

"Never mind. I know the language. I shall translate."

"Word for word, I beg you, word for word just this once.
I shall be eternally in your debt. No liberties—you must
understand . . . the weakness of my condition. My heart, it
simply won't support clouds and thunderclaps any more—"

"It is one sentence," he says.

"One sentence! Well, it must be a very *long* one."

He looks at her and narrows his eyes. They twinkle with
mischief and contempt. "No, Miss Rose, it is short," he

replies. "It says: 'I find the deceased, whose name is written above, to have died of his own stink.'" He smiles at her strangely.

Boober and I exchange a glance. Libby wrinkles his brow, bites his lower lip and regards Doberman suspiciously. Mr. Dew is whispering in the left ear of Miss Peduza, who is staring vacantly, with a bewildered, almost terrified expression on her face. Hanover Jones puts his hands in his pockets, hunches his shoulders up, stares at his feet and puckers his lips as though he has a need to whistle. Trembley mutters profane mysterious questions to himself: "What the pee? What the bloody hell?" etcetera. Weasel has a ferocious gleam in his eye. Even Ashe is taken aback. Pincher is the only one who doesn't seem the least bit fazed.

"You've done it again, haven't you, Mr. Doberman," says Miss Rose, quivering with rage. "That's not what the pathologist said at all, is it? You've gone ahead and given out one of your veils again, with an ugly name written on it. You are so fond of veils, of ugly names. Stink, you say? Street slang! What good is that, Mr. Doberman? What do you teach us by it? I beg you, let me have that piece of paper. Let me see it with my own eyes. If 'stink' in fact is what the fellow has written, then 'stink' it is, and you will have my apologies, I promise you. Well? What are you afraid of? An old hag like me? Come now, look at you. Look at you! Monster!"

She goes for him again, but again Pincher is there and holds her back, while Doberman takes out his little box of wooden matches and lights the edge of the paper. As it catches, he drops it near his feet, and everybody looks on in silence, watching it curl up and turn black. Miss Rose stares incredulous, uncomprehending, shuts her eyes briefly and then looks at Doberman with infinite disgust. "A madman," she mutters, hoarsely. "What—what a filthy little man—"

Boober goes to her and says, "Take heart, my dear."

She gets an arm loose and lets him have a swift one in the mouth; she is about to give him another when Pincher reasserts his hold.

"'Take heart'?" she says, agitated again. "From you? Phooey! You've been drinking, Boober. Drunkards, all of you, that's what you are! Every single one of you! I *too* can hand out ugly names, d'you see? Well you've left me my brain, anyway—thanks!—but you've burned up the place where it lives. Eh? I mean, Mr. Doberman, what good is that? I can't go on. D'you understand? Can't, can't! Bodkin, help me, my boy—"

"Let her go, Pincher," I say.

He lets her go and she takes my hand. "This one at least holds my hand," she says. She has worked herself into a sore throat now and is choking on every word. "At least he points no fingers. D'you see? At least he manages to keep his chin up. Eh, Mr. Libby? D'you see, Mr. Libby? I heard you before. You are a monkey. The whole circus. From my window. That sorrowful noise in the courtyard. I too am pointing fingers now, aren't I? But you leave me no choice, no choice! What a pass!"

SHEETS AND PHANTOMS

The party is reduced to confusion. Doberman escapes hastily into the little john near the file cabinet and locks the door, leaving the rest of us to our own devices. This is clever of him but cowardly. Everyone is on his feet. Ashe and Trembley rail at one another in a corner. Boober looks mournfully about the room. Weasel watches the door of the john, fiercely, and mutters to himself. Libby and Dew are joined in an effort to comfort Miss Peduza, who is crying without inhibition. Pincher and Hanover Jones take Miss

Rose out of the room; they each have one arm encircling her and one of her hands in theirs. I, seeing that this is an excellent opportunity to drift out, tag along behind them.

When they reach her room, "Scum and filth!" she cries, pushing them away and shutting the door in their faces.

Pincher goes downstairs to the office, but Handy says he will stand watch by her door for a bit. I slip away, across the yard to my sitting room. It is empty; the day counselor has left. He was supposed to stay on for two extra hours tonight while we had our meeting. He has left a note on the table. "Bodkin," it says, "cover up for me, will you? I got a date. The kids were asleep when I left." I crumple it up into the wastebasket and make a quick check of the beds.

Nod is awake still. He can't fall asleep, he says; he is afraid. Of a lot of things, and of Doberman in particular. He is afraid Doberman may come and kill him—"Like he done Page." I try to ease his mind, but it is not easy. Also, he sees ghosts: "They are out there in the sky. Sometimes they bang at the window glass."

"It's the wind," I tell him.

He is skeptical. "That ain't no wind."

And maybe it's not. After all, Ashe seems to see ghosts out there too. He calls them "phantoms" though. In fact, when you come down to it, according to Ashe, my whole justification for collecting a pay check depends on those phantoms. There is not much comfort in that.

"No," I say, looking out the window, "no ghosts out there at all, Nod. Not a one in the whole sky. Try and get some sleep, son."

But as I am going out the door, he again asks if I think he killed Page.

"You asked me that before, Nod. And I told you no, didn't I?"

"Yes . . ."

"Well then? What's wrong? Where'd you get such an idea? Did somebody say something to you? Did one of the kids here accuse you of killing Page . . . ? Is that what's bothering you?"

He is silent. "Did you say something?" I ask.

"Nothing."

"That *is* it then, isn't it? Somebody accused you of killing Page and got you all upset—right? Who was it?"

"Nobody," he says. "Never mind. That ain't it at all."

I shine my flashlight on the floor near his bed so I can see his face without glaring it in his eyes.

He props himself up on one elbow, squinting, and raises one hand as a shield. "Oh, now don't start with that flashlight, Body," he says amiably. "It hurts my eyes." He forces a smile, and as though he felt I needed to be comforted, says, "Don't worry about me. Forget what I said. I'm okay now. I just talk crazy sometimes. I'm going right to sleep, I promise."

I turn the flashlight off. "Okay."

"Good night, Bodkin."

Returning to my sitting room, I sink into my wonderful chair at last, slide my little book out of my pocket and attend to an appointment I made earlier with a certain chapter. But just as I am beginning to reacquaint myself with all my friends who lie under the print, voices fill the hall. Doberman and the watchmen, it sound like. Pincher too.

It is. They crowd in, breathing heavily; they are in a state. Why are they breathing heavily? Why are they in a state?

"Where is the day counselor?" says Doberman at once.

"I relieved him," I say.

"Relieved?"

"I told him to go on home. He had only fifteen more minutes to put in anyway, and he left just a minute ago. There was no need for him to stay on now that I'm here, was there?"

"But he is getting paid time and a *half* for these extra hours, Bodkin!" says Pincher, horrified.

"That does present a problem, doesn't it?" I say. "Administrative issues are infinite in their complexity, there's no getting away from it, Pincher . . . Won't you sit down, Mr. Doberman? Gentlemen?"

No, they prefer to stand, it seems. They are truly in a state.

"Why did you leave the office, Bodkin?" says Doberman, with a mixture of amusement and reproval—the sort of tone one might take with a child.

"Well, you dismissed us, didn't you, sir?" I say.

"Ah God, never mind. It is of no importance." He shakes his head.

"At any rate, sir," I say, "I think it was wonderfully self-effacing of you to come all the way from your office to my little sitting room. The mountain comes to Mohammed. I am flattered."

This he does not like. He looks at me sternly. "I am not a mountain, Bodkin. And you are not Mohammed. Keep that in mind. And wipe that grin off your face. We are here . . . simply because—"

"You wanted a breath of air, sir," says Pincher, giving me a wink on the sly, as if to say, "We must try to help the poor old fellow out in his dotage."

But Doberman turns on him angrily. "I do not need to be prompted, Mr. Pincher. I did not come here for a breath of air. I came expressly to Mr. Bodkin's sitting room with the others because I have something to say to them which is for their ears alone. Besides, the meeting adjourned with all of the principal issues unresolved."

"But that is precisely what I meant to say, sir!" says Pincher, showing us his palms. "That is . . . in short, a breath of air! I was speaking meta*phor*ically, sir—"

"And what were the principal issues, sir?" I say.

"There were several," says Doberman, glancing nervously about him at the other watchmen, who all avoid his eyes. "Number one: the spy business. You can forget about that, Bodkin. Until a few moments ago, I had no idea that Mr. Pincher had asked you to spy on your fellow watchmen here. It is a ludicrous idea, and had he told me about it, I should never have approved. Believe me," he adds, turning to the others, "I trust all of you implicitly. I hope none of you have had your feelings hurt."

He waits for them to say something, but they look at the floor.

"Now then," he continues, "number two: the autopsy."

"Ah yes, the autopsy, gentlemen!" says Pincher, beaming and rubbing his hands. "Mr. Doberman and I—that is to say, after a brief consultation with myself, Mr. Doberman has decided to make an *amend*ment to Dr. Sweeney's proposal in regards bedsheets."

"Why, sure!" says Trembley. "An amendment! Hah! What is it?"

Doberman looks at Pincher uncomfortably. "Why, Mr. Pincher, you and I had no consultation about the bedsheets."

But Pincher pretends not to have heard and, blithe and aery spirit that he is, presses on. "We shall no longer be changing the sheets once a week, as has been the custom. In light of the autopsy—"

"The autopsy," mutters Weasel.

"*In* light of the autopsy," continues Pincher, "we shall now be changing them every other day; that is, Monday, Wednesday and Friday."

In a small hoarse voice, Trembley invokes his grandfather and shuts his eyes. The others too are impressed.

"So now," continues Pincher, "the innovation is not, in effect, merely to increase the esprit de corps of the watchmen; it will be of palpable financial assistance as well. We simply cannot afford a laundry bill for three linen changes a week."

"Then why have the three changes in the first place?" says Trembley, his dander up.

"Because of the autopsy, Mr. Trembley," says Pincher, closing his eyes for a moment at the spectacle of Trembley's stupidity. "When a child dies of his own stink, the institution clearly must take sanitary measures at once!"

Doberman is astonished. "Don't tell me, Mr. Pincher, that you actually believe—"

But Pincher is in a transport, carried away on the wave of his own ideas, and he ignores Doberman. "Furthermore, I have received a communication tonight from Dr. Sweeney himself. He wants to interview the five of you while you are washing the sheets. He is interested in keeping a record, you see, of your reactions. He would like to discover a pattern. And rest assured, gentlemen, that he *will* discover a pattern! He will be making these interviews periodically, once every two weeks."

"Now *there's* a scientific fellow for you," says Trembley. He taps his forefinger on Pincher's lapel. "I can only take

my hat off to him. Well, sir, I will try to be bright and gay
during his interview of me at the tub. I'll try to think of the
stuff in a pretty way even. Just for him! Linens for loonies?
No, now that'll never do. Better *wings*—that's it—the wings
of Ashe's angels here. What d'you say, lads? Nice, eh? That
ought to impress him, don't you think?"

"*Mis*ter Trembley," says Doberman, "there is something
you don't understand. In fact, there is something that apparently none of you understand."

But nothing of what Doberman has begun to say regis-
ters. Trembley widens his bloodshot eyes, thrusts his hands
in his trouser pockets and hunches his shoulders up to his
ears. "Well, I don't want the doctor to feel guilty about
laying this job on my back, do I?" he says, suddenly full of
contrition, the anger rising up in his face. "No, I tell you,
Pincher, I'd like to ease his mind. I'd like to say to him,
'Now, don't you worry your head about this one bit, Doctor, because I bet I don't feel half as bad about this job
you've laid on me as you must feel in having to lay it on me
in the first place. In fact, I sort of like it. It's all in the
interest of science, ain't it? And if there's ever any way I
can be of interest to science, why, I'm glad to be it!' And if
there's ever a thing he can figure up for the two nights when
there's no laundry, just go ahead and tell him from me,
Pincher, that I, for one, am in a cooperative sweat."

"That will do, Mr. Trembley," says Doberman.

"Do, sir? Do? But I ain't done anything hardly!"

"I must ask you to be silent at once."

"Maybe the good doctor would even be so kind as to
cooperate with *me!* Know what I mean? I mean, maybe in
exchange for all my scrubbing, he'd oblige me with a certified medical explanation of that burnt-up *au*topsy of yours!

*Au*topsy! Hah! Sure! Because I got a dull mind, sir, and it don't catch *on* too quick. See?"

He takes his whiskey bottle out of his coat pocket, tosses off a long draft and defiantly wipes his lips with his forearm. I have never seen him display his bottle in Doberman's presence, though of course Doberman has always known that Trembley drinks on the job and everywhere else.

Doberman looks at the floor and begins to speak, but Pincher interrupts him again. "The autopsy, gentlemen, is a matter—"

"For God's sake, Mr. Pincher," says Doberman unhappily, "be still for one moment and let me speak."

"Forgive me, sir. It was my intention only to be of service, and to legislate and reorganize . . . in short, to clarify—"

"Never mind!" cries Doberman through his teeth, his eyes squeezed shut in exasperation. Then he smiles wanly and tries to recompose himself. "Listen to me, all of you. I would like to clear up a few misunderstandings here. First, let me dispel any anxiety you have in regards the nature of Page's death. The autopsy—and I will speak about the contents of it in a moment—the autopsy makes it clear beyond a doubt that we are *not,* I repeat *not,* involved in a murder case here—"

"The autopsy make nothing clear," mutters Weasel.

"What, Mr. Weasel?" says Doberman.

"I said, 'The autopsy.'"

"What about it?"

"It make nothing clear!"

"I don't follow you."

"He don't follow." Weasel turns to me and points his finger at Doberman. "See, Jew? He don't follow. What do that mean, hum?"

I shrug my shoulders. I am uneasy. Weasel clenches his fists and looks about for something to exercise them on, but there is nothing except me and the others.

"What do that mean!" he shouts at Doberman, who takes a step backward instinctively. "It mean nothing! Nothing mean nothing! What is that stink you talking about? Hum? What! I want to know. The Weasel he wants to know."

"Mr. Weasel, I am afraid that—"

"You afraid is right. What do you take us for? Hum? Dopes?"

"Not at all."

"You must be losing your beans, Mr. Doberman, I tell you plain. Do you think there was ever a body that will believe such a lie as 'stink'? Hum? No sir. Never. Now, you listen to me. I want to know *what* that paper say. And I want to know it *now*. And I want to know it *clear*. And I want to know it with no buts about it!"

"Well, I am trying to tell you, Mr. Weasel," says Doberman gently. "Why . . . why, I am astonished at all of you! 'Of his own stink' . . . that was an obvious lie, of course. It never entered my head to deceive you with it. I thought you all would understand that what I said was purely for the benefit of Miss Rose—!"

There is a moment of silence, then "You didn't intend to deceive us, sir?" says Trembley. He scratches his head.

"Of course not!" says Doberman, smiling broadly.

"Then what *do* it say?" says Weasel, stamping his foot.

"If you can be patient for a moment, Mr. Weasel, I shall tell you. What time do you have, Mr. Pincher?"

"You mean to say that Page did *not* die of his own stink, sir?" says Pincher, and in great agitation he looks at his watch. "Five minutes after eleven, sir. No, forgive me, *four* minutes."

"Oh?" Doberman narrows his eyes. "Well, I see we are running a little late. Would you be so kind as to inform the counselors in the other wards that we will require their services until eleven-thirty? I'd like to speak to the watchmen for a while longer."

"It won't be necessary, sir," says Pincher, looking worried. "They will stay until they are relieved. Besides, I am anxious to learn the nature of the autopsy myself."

Doberman glances quickly at Weasel, to make sure he is still at bay. "Mr. Pincher, do as I tell you, and do it at once. And when you return, please knock before entering."

Pincher is amazed. He begins to speak, but bites his lower lip and walks to the door. He turns back after opening it. "You do intend to tell me about the autopsy, sir . . . don't you?"

"Perhaps." Doberman doesn't look at him.

"Sir!" says Pincher, throwing up his hands. "What can this mean? Am I to take it that you no longer *trust* me? *Me?* Robert Pincher? Is that how I am to take it, sir?"

"You may take it any way you like. Please shut the door; I am getting a chill. Wait—one thing before you go. I want you to inform Dr. Sweeney that the bedsheet proposal has been rejected by me. And furthermore, I don't want you even to *men*tion the word 'bedsheet' to these gentlemen— ever again! The whole idea is a complete insanity. Now you may go, Pincher. Well? Don't just stand there gaping, man! Shut the door!"

Pincher looks at us watchmen as though expecting us to extend him our sympathy. He knows that none of us are about to, yet he seems to expect it of us, which only makes him appear more ridiculous. Were Weasel not in such a passion, he might be sympathetic—but he is in a passion.

Pincher is quite alone. He blinks, looks at Doberman with childlike wonder, and goes out the door backward, closing it meticulously, his large clumsy body bent over the door-knob. The latch clicks, and there is a heavy silence in the room. I almost regret that he has left.

But in a minute he appears at the windowpane, his nose pressed against it, his eyes darting about inquisitively. He meets Doberman's eyes, gapes in embarrassment, fogs up the glass with his breath and then flies away across the yard. A light snow is falling.

"Let us sit down, gentlemen," says Doberman with a conspiratorial air, almost in a whisper. "Come, let us sit down together. We haven't much time."

We each pull up a folding chair to the table, and Doberman rests his forearms on the top and leans forward. "Now, this is a very serious matter, gentlemen. Do we understand? I must have your word that nothing of what I am about to tell you will go beyond this room."

He examines our faces. We nod our heads and mutter—though not in the most friendly or reassuring manner—to indicate that we will keep the secret. He seems disappointed—he would have liked a happier show of good faith—but he has already launched himself and there is no turning back. Besides, it would appear that he is as eager now to have the secret off his chest as we are to learn it.

"The autopsy was vague, gentlemen," he says. "It was not in Latin, of course, but in standard medical language. It was long and involved—a complete fiasco, the kind of autopsy a pathologist will compose when the cause of death is absolutely indeterminate. Miss Rose would have recognized the type at once."

"But why did you lie then, sir?" I say.

"Why?" he says. "Because Miss Rose is in a state. You heard her, didn't you? 'One atom of reasonableness,' she said. Do you see? Another uncertainty, like that autopsy, and we would have seen her transformed into a babbling idiot."

"So you wanted to give her something certain, is that the idea?" says Trembley, squinting at Doberman's face as if it were a Chinese puzzle.

"I don't understand," says Weasel, his eyes shifting back and forth nervously. "Stink . . . I don't understand 'stink'!"

"Patience, Mr. Weasel," says Doberman. "I'm getting to it . . . So once I had looked over the autopsy, I thought that the best idea would be simply to fold up the paper and tell Miss Rose that it was rather a long report, but that it could be summed up in the phrase 'heart failure.' She probably would have taken offence at the vulgarity of the term and had a tantrum, but in the end would have contented herself with it as a suitable, if rather general, answer. However, when I looked at her, all of a sudden I felt mischievous. That's all . . . do you see? It was pure mischief, Mr. Weasel. I thought you all had understood that! At first I wanted to help her out—and then a little voice inside me said, 'Doberman, how many insults have you endured in silence from this wretched woman? And for how many years!'"

Weasel isn't amused. His lower lip quivers with rage. "And what you going to tell these little boys tomorrow? Hum? Stink? They ain't going to like that, I can tell you."

"No, of course not. I shall tell them 'heart failure.' Because they too, like Miss Rose, cannot stand any more uncertainty in their lives. Otherwise they would imagine all sorts of nonsense. No, they must have something certain."

"That's right," says Weasel. "Because they is a lot of little boys here what think *you* done it, Mr. Doberman."

Doberman pretends not to have heard this. "Something certain, yes. So you can see why I dismissed Mr. Pincher from the room. In the past he has proved himself a very poor confidant. Along with Miss Rose and everyone else at Ulser, he is to be told 'heart failure'—and there it will end."

There is a knock at the door. "M-May I come in, sir?" says Pincher, with a theatrical shiver in his voice.

"No, you may not!" shouts Doberman. "Wait there until I call you."

Weasel, who has been grinding his jaw muscles ever since Pincher's departure, pounds his fist once on the table, rises from his chair, walks across the room and stands by the door.

Doberman glances at him fearfully for a moment, then attempts to ignore him. "Tomorrow I am retiring Miss Rose from her position. I thought you should know of this, gentlemen. I would like you to listen at her door once on the hour tonight. You may take turns. I have a feeling she may be running about again."

"The poor woman!" says Ashe. "What ever will she do with herself now?"

"That is not my concern, Mr. Ashe. She has served seventeen years. She is entitled to a two-thousand-dollar retirement bonus. And there it will end. She is no longer of use."

"That's right," says Weasel, leaning against the doorpost, his arms folded across his chest. "And I will be glad to see that old Jewish witch out of my sight."

Doberman looks at me and then turns around in his chair to face Weasel. "I'm sorry, Mr. Weasel, but I'm afraid that your remark was not in the best taste."

Weasel narrows his eyes. "No. But 'stink' now—that is real tasty, I guess. Oh sure. You tell me what is tasty and what is not tasty. But I know what is what here now. I know."

"Then please tell me!" Doberman rises from his chair suddenly and walks across the room, with his back to Weasel. Into a corner, as though there were someone there, he says, "What, Mr. Weasel, is what—?"

"Black and white—that is what is what," says Weasel.

Doberman turns around and glares at him. "What do you mean?" he says emphatically, tightening his lips. But he knows very well what Weasel means.

"I mean 'stink.' I mean you would never say that if it was a white child. I know. And you would never do a white man like you did Pincher. You would never put a white man in the cold like that. But I know why. Pincher he is too close to the top, so he got to stay in the cold. Lest he find out too much. You got to keep him down. Because if you don't keep him down, then pretty soon there will be a black man on top. And you don't like that."

"First of all," says Doberman, "Page was half white."

"There is no half white. Half white is nigger anyplace you go. So don't give me that 'half white'!"

"I should like to end this discussion at once, Mr. Weasel."

"Sure. You end it. But first you hear me out. Mischief or no mischief, I don't like what you say about that child. 'Stink'—that is ugly. Miss Rose is right. You love ugly names. All his life little Page have ugly names on top of him. Least when he die, let him be. Let him have a fine word to bury him with. But you think: No. Page has no mama or papa. I can do him like I like.

"But listen here: you wrong. He *has* a papa. *Wea*sel *he* is the papa. Of all these little boys here! And the Weasel he take *ex-cep-tion* to what you say!"

"Fine, but . . . there are certain complications which you totally—"

"Fine nothing! Sure now. Complications. I bet they is. Because wherever is Mr. Doberman, there you will find complications. Right, brothers? Sure. We know that. I been a long time in this hell. But now we have a different time. The Weasel he is now at the end of the rope. He tired. And justice along with him tired. What are we tired *of*? We tired of the end of the rope. See? For a long time now I have never spoke up to you. I respect you. I come when you say come. I go when you say go. I protect your name amongst the little children. I keep peace in the night, and I punch my clock. And why? Because all the time I think to myself: This place is hard. But it a place. And these is children what need a place. And Mr. Doberman? He is the boss. And his job is hard. Because the place is hard. Someday he will know it be *too* hard. Then he will leave. And then a black man will be boss again. Like in the old times, like old Lyle. Lyle now—he knew a thing or two about what is what! But don't worry. There will be a black boss again by and by. I just got to bide my time.

"And so I do. Because why? Because the Weasel love these children. That is why he beat them. Just like Lyle did! He beat them to make them *strong* so that they grow up to be something fine. He don't want to see them grow up to be street cleaners and bums and . . . and night watch-mens! And when they die, he don't want to see them be called a 'stink' . . ."

"That is all well and good, Mr. Weasel," says Doberman uneasily. "However, let me give you fair warning—"

"Sure, you give me fair warning. But first I give *you* fair warning. And you going to hear me out, lest I tie you to a chair and *make* you hear me out."

"My dear brother," begins Ashe.

"Stay out, nigger," says Weasel, not bothering to take his eyes off Doberman. Tears have sprung into Weasel's eyes, but he refuses to acknowledge them; perhaps he is even unaware of them. "Now, I know, Mr. Doberman, that you ain't got no worries about the Page's mama and papa. Because the mama is dead, and the papa, nobody know who that white man is. But I tell you, you got worries with Weasel, and you got to *count* to him. Because he love these children like his own sons, all of them. There isn't a one I haven't given a licking to least twice. You know what Page say when I give him a licking? He say, 'You the only one what care, Mr. Weasel. Because you give us a whipping when we are bad. I will be good from here on out.' And he was. Wasn't he good? Sure! So you got to count to me, see? Because I got a powerful interest in that child. I got my mark on him, Mr. Doberman. And he take that mark with him to the grave."

"But my dear brother," says Ashe, mournfully, "what is it that you want from Mr. Doberman?"

"What I want? I want an apology! No . . . no! *Page* wants an apology. And I come to get it for him so he can rest in peace!"

The tears are sliding down his face, and veins swell in his throat.

Trembley, Boober and Ashe look away from him uneasily; for once in their lives they are sensible enough to
keep their mouths shut. It is clear to everyone in the room,
even to Weasel himself, that one wrong word will set him
off and then rhetoric will no longer suffice, and there will be
a fury to reckon with.

Doberman has put his hands in his trouser pockets and is
looking down at the toe of one foot nervously sliding
around in a small circle. He says, "Well, of course . . . of
course you have my apologies. Believe me, Mr. Weasel, I
had no intention whatsoever of profaning the death of that
innocent child. In fact, I had no in*tenti*on of saying it at all.
I thought I had made that clear to you, but obviously I
didn't. It just seemed to escape from me . . . do you understand? Like a little devil that simply had to leap out of
me."

"You don't have to talk to me like I was a child," says
Weasel. "I know what 'intention' mean."

"I wasn't talking to you as if you were a child," says
Doberman despairingly. "I am fond of figures. I *oft*en express myself in figures."

"In *what?*" says Weasel.

"Fig— Ah God, never mind!" Doberman hits the wall
feebly with the side of his fist, and tears spring into his eyes
too. He, Weasel and Boober have tears at present. If
Trembley, Ashe and I can remain clear-eyed, perhaps a
reasonable balance will be maintained.

"Don't nobody be banging their fist at me!" says Weasel.

"I was not banging my fist at *you,* Mr. Weasel," says
Doberman.

"Don't tell *me* who you banging your fist at. *I* know what
is what here."

[127]

"Then suppose you tell me," says Doberman with melancholy, letting his shoulders droop, his arms hang loosely, "What, Mr. Weasel, is what? Hm?"

"Black and white! That is what is what!" shouts Weasel. But he has shouted that before, and now it sounds lost, like a dog falling and barking in a bottomless pit. And it makes Weasel even angrier to hear his voice falling through the darkness like that.

Doberman walks wearily back to his chair and eases himself into it. "You have made your point, Mr. Weasel. Believe me, I understand you."

"You don't understand nothing . . ."

"Now, I have only one thing further to say to you," continues Doberman with determination. "You spoke of 'lickings.' There are to be no more of them. Is that clear? Since I took office six years ago, it has been the policy of this institution to forbid physical punishment. That has been the policy, yes. Now, Mr. Weasel, from this day forth, it will be the *prac*tice as well. Is that clear?"

There go Weasel's jaw muscles again. He reaches into the rear pocket of his trousers, pulls out a handkerchief and brings it up to his face to wipe away the tears. But immediately he changes his mind and wipes his brow instead. He stuffs the handkerchief back in his pocket, bends to one side and spits on the floor.

Ashe gasps for God's mercy. Trembley mutters something, none of which is discernible except "nigger," Boober closes his eyes and shakes his head, and Weasel bolts out the door, slamming it behind him.

It opens again immediately and Pincher puts his head in the room. "M-May I come in now, sir?"

Doberman sighs and Pincher tiptoes in, shutting the door

quietly. There is a reverent silence in the room, which has been caused by the very sad look on Doberman's face. He is slumped in his chair, his hands hanging loosely between his knees. Boober, Trembley and Ashe take Pincher into a corner and whisper at him.

A few minutes go by like this.

"May I venture to speak, Mr. Doberman?" says Pincher, bending forward at the waist.

Doberman closes his eyes and nods.

"Mr. Trembley, Mr. Ashe and Mr. Boober, sir, have filled me in," says Pincher. "And I must tell you, sir, that I had always suspected that the child was not quite right in the heart. One could see it in his fingernails, sir . . ."

"I'm tired," says Doberman abstractedly. "I'm going home."

"Ah, but one question, sir, before you go," says Pincher. Doberman rises from his chair wearily and smiles at Pincher with pity. "Well?"

"There is yet another issue, which . . . that is to say, so far as I can make out from what these gentlemen have told me of the proceedings of the meeting—another issue, sir, which is yet unresolved."

"And what is that?"

"Mr. Bodkin, sir. What do you propose to do about him? That is to say, sir, I thought Mr. Libby's arguments quite convincing."

"I see. Well, I am afraid I myself did not."

"But Mr. Libby has threatened to resign! And he will, sir. He is a man of principle. He has a great intellect. An outstanding scholastic background. If Mr. Bodkin doesn't leave, then Mr. Libby will. What shall we do?"

Doberman sits down on the table and lets his legs dangle

over the edge like a little boy. "Do? Well, there is nothing
we can do. If Mr. Libby wants to resign, then he may
resign. I have no hold on him, I cannot force him to stay.
Besides, the question doesn't interest me in the least. Do
you understand me? Only one thing interests me now: that
we begin to straighten out the administration. One hopes
therefore that this little catastrophe may have shaken a few
consciences. So you see, I am glad that Mr. Libby's conscience has been moved. But beyond that? Listen to me,
Pincher. I would like things to *change* here. I would like the
brutality to cease and the foolish arguments to be resolved.
I would like that little child not to have died entirely in
vain. Little Benjamin Page . . . why, I am no longer even
sure whether or not there ever was such a child. Was there?
One can no longer prove satisfactorily that there was.
Where is he? I cannot see him. But I see all these other little
boys here. I see them and I think to myself: Here one can
do something. They are not phantoms, do you see, Pincher?"

"With perfect clarity, sir!" cries Pincher, who is obviously moved to the depths of delight. "You express yourself
so well, sir. I understand you perfectly. You are giving us
another variation on your parable of the packet of seeds.
The creature must grow outward—isn't that the idea, sir?"

"Yes . . ." Doberman blushes with shame. Why does he
blush with shame? Because it is true; Pincher really does
understand. And if Pincher understands—well then, of
what value can Doberman's ideas possibly be? Pincher
serves a useful function. He prevents Doberman from
committing the sin of pride. No sooner has Doberman given
voice to what he thought was a lofty sentiment, than
Pincher gives it back to him word for word. Then Doberman thinks to himself: What am I, after all? I'm a Pincher
—no, worse: I am a Doberman.

Now he dismisses everyone but me from the room, and when we are alone he says, "Bodkin, tomorrow I am firing Weasel. I cannot allow that kind of behavior. He has become unmanageable. I would like to fire him tonight, but I wouldn't dare. He is ready to explode. Keep an eye on him, will you?"

"Yes, sir."

We walk out into the hall together. Doberman opens the outer door a crack. The wind whistles, and snowflakes whirl in around his legs. He turns up the collar of his coat. The hall is poorly lit and the shadows on his face make him look very old. He shudders at the prospect of going out.

"It's a slaughterhouse, this place," he says hollowly. "The court . . . they send the souls of children here for slaughter—and for slaughter alone . . . that's the long and the short of it. Well? And what do you call a man who presides over such a place?"

"Come now, sir—you're in one of your moods again. What you need is a good night's rest."

He smiles at me and puts one hand on my shoulder affectionately. "Of course . . . a good night's rest . . . you're a fine young man . . ." He fastens the top button of his coat and pulls the brim of his hat down a little further over his brow. "Oh yes, one other thing. The time clock . . . you will punch in on the half-hour from now on, won't you? It would make things so much simpler."

"Yes, sir, I will."

"Good. Things are going to improve, wait and see. Good night, Bodkin." He goes out the door with one arm across his face to block the wind and snow.

I punch the clocks in the hall and have a look at the beds, all of which save one are occupied. Returning to my sitting room, I take my book out of my pocket and caress the binding—a sly ritual, and a somewhat questionable habit when one comes down to it.

What I ought to do right now is call up Belle Jones. She is Doberman's secretary. She files and fabulates. She is alabaster and warm. Her bosom is exquisite. Her hair shines. It is long and black. And when she moves . . . oh, Bodkin, when she moves . . .

I will call her up on the telephone. I will go down to my sitting room right now and call her up. "Come on over," I will tell her. "Quick. There's an empty bed. Nobody is around. What do you say? I need to see you. I'm at a juncture. But I'll smile straightway you climb in the window. I'll amuse you with legends—please!—stand on my hands, kiss the balls of your feet, roll you over a thousand delights. Say yes, Belle—yes, yes, yes! Say it."

And then she will breathe heavily into the receiver, and her irrepressible "Yes" will wake up every little bird asleep along the wires between us.

After we hang up, I will brood awhile in sweet anticipation. I will take my shoes off and float up to the third floor to wait for her. If any of the boys awakes, I will gag him and tie him up in a closet. I will sit on the window sill and try to imitate Boober, work up a high, magnificent melancholy. I am not as good at it as I used to be, but I will manage, all the same.

At last I will hear her heels on the fire escape and quietly raise the window. "Careful, Belle. It's icy. Take it slow."

"Body," she will whisper from the second landing, "I love you. And this better convince you. Does it?"

"Well, I tell you, old girl, it convinces me just halfway. One more flight though, and you'll have my whole conviction in your lap. Word of honor."

And then up she will come, and I will lift her through the window and hold her in my arms and . . . ah God, there is a noise overhead on the third floor. A lot of footsteps. They are whispering up there excitedly. I go into the vestibule and listen for a moment. They saw a movie tonight in the gymnasium, and that usually puts them up in the air. I was surprised that it was so quiet when I first came on. The third floor is Libby's group—Page's. What is it they are saying? I tiptoe up about three steps and listen.

"We going to go down there and kill them." That is Punzel's voice; he is the biggest of the group and the acknowledged leader. "You six will take Blinken. And the rest of us will take Nod."

"Are you sure, man?"

"Am I sure what?"

"That they kill the Page?"

"What's the matter, boy? You scared? Sure I'm sure."

"Shh."

They lower their voices so that I can't make out what they are saying. I was right, then. Just as I thought, this was what Nod was upset about. But can they really believe that he and Blinken killed Page? I creep up a few more steps until I am high enough to hear what they are saying; maybe I can find out what's at the bottom of it. I go very slowly and make sure no boards creak. But by the time I'm where I can hear them, they have changed the subject on me.

"Them two, did they make babies tonight in that movie?" says little Wimsy, who arrived only a month ago and is the youngest in the group.

"Yeah."

"Where was it?"

"Where's what, stupid?"

"The baby they made."

"Ha, ha, ha ..."

"It *is* still in that lady's belly," says Punzel. "It takes years and years to come out. It don't just pop out like that."

"How many years?"

"Ten years. More sometimes."

"I mean, but how do they do it?"

"Tell him, tell him," say a lot of them at once, joyfully.

"Okay," says Punzel. "See, Wimsy—Mr. Rock Hudson he takes that lady's buns, that's how they do it."

"How come he want to make babies?"

"Because he likes her buns."

"Is that how come you are taking my buns, Punzel?" says Wimsy.

"Yeah."

"You making babies in my buns?"

"Yeah."

"Ha, ha, ha, ha ..."

"What am I to do with them babies!" cries Wimsy. "Mama, help me—"

"Stop crying, stupid."

"You just send your babies to this place, Wimsy. But you have time. Years and years. Ha, ha."

"Don't fret, Wimsy," says Fergus, the scholar of the group. "He's jiving you. You have no babies in you. Only womens have babies."

"Yeah?"

"This Sunday, Wimsy, you come and sit with me in the church," says Punzel. "And we will pray God He don't give you no babies, like the Rock give that lady."

"Do God give babies? I thought the buns give babies."

"Ha, ha, ha . . ."

"Stupid!" says Punzel. "God makes everything, don't He? Well, He makes your buns and your babies too."

"How come?"

"How come! Because He God, that is how come."

"You are stupid, Wimsy. You got to pray God to give you smarts," adds Fergus. He is, in short, scholarly, but disinterested.

"Never mind about it," says Punzel. "God don't listen to the likes of Wimsy."

"He do!" cries Wimsy.

"He don't. Because you don't *love* God. You love buns and that's all. And who that love buns hate God."

"I don't!"

"You do. You hate God, Wimsy. You bad. I'm going to do you tonight real bad."

"No, no, don't hurt me . . ."

"Ha, ha, ha . . ."

"You terrible."

"I'll tell!"

"Who? Who will you tell?"

"God," says Wimsy.

"He don't listen to wicked Wimsies."

"He do!"

"He don't."

"I'll tell Doberman."

"He don't neither. He laugh."

"Bodkin . . . *he* hears. *He* knows."

"He can't do nothing. He is a Jew."

"Ha, ha, ha . . ."

"I'll tell Dr. Sweeney!"

"Him?" says Punzel. "Oh boy. Go ahead. You know what he say. He say, 'Boy, you neurotic and psychotic. You act out, you is hostility and crazy. You fitty as a faggit. You rationalize your masturbation, and God is what you make Him.' He is an atheist and a white mother-fucker. He laugh, that's all."

I start up the stairs, stamping my feet heavily to frighten them back into bed before I get there. They fear my footsteps more than me, and I have to make the best of what I have. I hear them scatter and dive, and by the time I enter the bedroom they are all buried under their blankets.

"I want quiet up here," I say.

They giggle under their blankets and into their pillows.

"Punzel?" I say.

He pulls the blanket off his head. "Yeah, Mr. Jewish Bodykin?"

He laughs, and the others laugh too and pull their blankets off their heads. What do I do now?

"Are you okay, Wimsy?" I say.

"Yeah, Mr. Jewish," he answers.

This also brings a round of laughter. I shine my light in little Wimsy's face. He is smiling at me broadly. The look of his face shining in the little circle of light in the dark room delights everyone, and they laugh again, but more sincerely. Even I can't resist a smile. The boy has a ridiculously happy, handsome, though somehow comical face. Still, I am offended by it. How am I to protect him if he assumes an attitude like that? Here I am, ready to take up arms against the diabolical forces that have risen up against him in the night, and he sits there and smiles at me.

"We just having a little fun up here," he explains, and then he laughs quite genuinely, with a conspiratorial wink

at Fergus, who is in the next bed. Winks and laughs. Okay.
I turn off my flashlight. I look over toward Punzel's bed. I
can barely see him in the dark.

"What is it I heard you say about Nod before, Punzel?"

"Nothing," he says.

"Nothing my foot. I heard you. You might as well own
up."

"He killed the Page, that's what I said . . . so what about
it?"

"Do you really believe that?" I say. "And the rest of you?
You believe it too?"

They all start in to whisper at me at once:

"He done it."

"You bet, Bodkin."

"That little faggit, he killed the Page, all right."

"That's enough," I say. I take a step toward Punzel's
bed. "What makes you think that Nod killed Page?"

"Think nothing, man. I *know*."

"That's about the craziest thing I've heard in the nine
years I've been here, Punzel. Do you think that a boy who
did what Nod did the other day could have murdered Page
in his sleep? That took a great deal of courage—to sit down
in the snow like that. Do you know that?"

"Courage!" says Punzel. "That ain't courage. That is
guilt *feel*ing. You ask Dr. Sweeney about courage. He will
tell you all about courage. Guilt *feel*ing is what he say."

"Guilt? What's Nod got to feel guilty about?"

"Murder, man. He kill the Page, didn't he? Well then? So
then he sit his buns down in the snow. See? So he hurt
himself a little. And then after he hurt himself a little, he
don't feel guilty no more."

I look around and glance at all the beds, but I can't see

any faces clearly. "Is that what all of you believe, then?"

"You bet, Mr. Bodkin."

"Yeah, it is the truth."

"That little faggit, he kill the Page, all right."

"And we going to do him in, you wait and see."

"Quiet down, all of you," I say. "Punzel, tell me something. What makes you think Nod would want to kill Page?" I flick on my flashlight and shine it at him. "Well?"

"Get that fucking light out of my eye and I will tell you," he says. "Okay now. That Nod, see—and Blinken too—they took little Page in the closet with them one day. See? A couple weeks ago. And Page he holler something terrible. So we all of us run down there, see. The whole group of us. We stick together. We run down there and we beat up on those two little faggits. Do you get it now? Huh? Do you get me?"

"No. No, I don't."

"They want to get *even!* See? Them two little faggits want to get even! Because we beat up on them! *Even!* So they got even, all right. They kill the Page. Now they are even, and pretty soon they are going to be dead too. Even and dead. Right, men?"

"Yeah, yeah . . ."

"Even and dead."

"Even and dead, even and dead!"

"We going to kill them, you bet."

"Nobody is killing anybody," I say. "Pipe down. I've heard enough. You'll wake up the whole place."

"What's the matter, Jewish man? You scared?"

"He scared everybody going to wake up and kill his ass. Right, Jew?"

They start in. A couple of them get out of bed and dance

in circles with their arms linked. The others rise up too.
They throw pillows. They laugh. They sing and clap their
hands. They each sing a different song. The words are in-
genious insults in rhyme aimed at me. 'Jew' and 'Bodkin'
are melodious words, and one can improvise on them for a
long time with a minimum of effort. I admonish them and
throw them one by one back into bed, and one by one they
jump out again.

Presently Weasel's unmistakable footsteps are heard coming up the stairs. He wears a heavy shoe. It is recognized at
once, that shoe, and they dive into their beds and bury
themselves in the covers.

It seems that about two or three times every year, without fail, I forget myself and take on a conversation with too
many boys at once, and overextend it, and then a riot gets
under way. On these occasions it has always been Weasel
who has come to get me out of it. He sits in his room across
the yard and listens attentively. If not for him, perhaps I
would have been out of a job long ago. He has been good
about it for the most part; he has come to accept my nature
over the years and is usually decent enough to spare me
open contempt in this matter.

His eyes are ablaze as he appears at my side in the room.
"What is all that racket up here?" he says to the boys, and
touches my elbow gently as if to say, "Don't worry, dear
friend. Everything's all right now."

"Punzel," he says, "is that your voice I hear from all the
way cross the yard? Hum?"

There is no answer, and I whisper to Weasel, "That's
okay, let it go. They'll be quiet now."

"No, Jew," he whispers, "we don't let it go. That is the
Weasel's whole secret."

He walks to Punzel's bed and pulls him up onto his feet by the ear. "Now, boy, come up and get your justice."

He gives him two strokes of the belt across the backside, and then Weasel and I go on down the stairs together, his arm around my shoulder.

Standing in the vestibule at the foot of the stairs, he peers at me and says, "What's the matter? You don't look happy."

"Oh, but I am. I'm happy." And I am. After all, why shouldn't I be?

"Go on and get your coat. We will step into the cold air for a trifle and have a smoke."

So I get my coat and we step outside. He offers me one of his cigarettes, and we smoke in silence. The flurry of snow that had been falling a few minutes ago has ended, and now the air is clear and much colder.

Weasel finishes his cigarette and flicks it across the yard. "You look better now," he says. "You got to slow down, that is the main thing. I know you a long time now, and I can tell by your eyes, Jew, when your brain go too fast."

He lights himself another cigarette and peers at me over the flame cupped in his hand. "You are not worried about what that Libby said about you . . . are you, Jew?"

"No."

"Good," he says, throwing the match away, "because he is a lunatic. You are no murderer, Jew. This is justice himself speaking to you, and I speak plain. Okay?"

"Sure."

"Good. See you at breakfast—"

"Wait," I say. "There's one thing. About Nod. Those boys up there in Page's group, Punzel and the rest—they think that Nod killed him, that Nod killed Page . . ."

"They do, do they," he says, laughing heartily, but he puts one hand on his ribs.

"Yes."

He stops laughing and looks down at his feet, still smiling though, and shakes his head philosophically. Then he touches my arm and says with affection, "Listen to me, Jew. Go on back inside and read your book. I will see you at breakfast." He walks away, shaking his head and laughing softly to himself, and disappears into the building.

I stand out in the cold for a while longer and then repair to my sitting room, where it is warm and very quiet. For the rest of the night, I sit in my chair and read and punch the clocks on the half-hour. I don't leave my quarters at all— except just once. Around one A.M. I get a pang of conscience about Weasel; I think that maybe I ought to go over and tell him that Doberman intends to fire him. I walk across the yard and peer through the window of Weasel's sitting room. He has three sleepy boys standing at attention around his table. Sitting at the far side of the room, his chair tilted back against the wall, is Pincher. He has a book in his hand and is reading aloud. Every other minute he pauses, and then Weasel shuts his eyes and recites. Edna St. Vincent Millay is what they're at tonight. Weasel gives a new slant to those rapturous lines. It is like an elephant waltzing to Strauss. That's right, I forgot—tonight is Wednesday. Every Wednesday, Pincher gives Weasel a "culture lesson," as they call it. It has been going on for a few months now and seems to be working out nicely. I told Pincher when he first took up the enterprise that I thought it was a decent and selfless thing for him to do—whereupon he looked at me in amazement and replied, "But he's paying me five dollars a lesson, Bodkin!" Pincher has his humility, you see, though it is of a special kind, and one has to have an eye for the devious to locate it. At the end of the third line in the second quatrain of a sonnet Weasel pokes one of the boys, who is beginning to fall asleep, in the ribs, and then proceeds to the fourth line.

I have a change of heart and head back across the yard. Midway I encounter Boober, who has come out to look for me. Just a moment ago during a bed check he found a scalpel lying beside a pillow. He shows it to me unhappily. Obviously the boy stole it out of the infirmary and hid it under his pillow, from which it slipped out during the night. A common enough occurrence, but it never fails to be upsetting. We talk about it out in the cold, and I tell him why I came out and about Weasel's being fired tomorrow.

He peers through Weasel's window for a moment then turns back to me and looks into my eyes in silence.

"So Weasel is to be fired," he says at last. He smiles sadly. "Well, well . . . and you are troubled, I see. I understand. I too am troubled. There is no question, Bodkin, but that there is an alliance between ourselves and Weasel . . . which is founded upon his talent for whipping little boys. I shall be sorry to see him go. What if another weeper like me, or another bookish Jew like you, moves into his place? Then we shall have to whip the little boys ourselves. But we have no talent in that line. We shall have to practice. Alliances are simpler. And when they are founded upon an equitable assignation of talent, they are even clever. I'm having trouble lately—with my kidneys, I think—right here . . . there's a pain . . . do you know a good doctor, Bodkin?"

MORNING

The Days on my ward arrive at seven-thirty. They come into the sitting room to collect their keys from me. I tell them about the little conspiracy against Nod which is brewing in Group Three. Libby, who is in charge of that group this morning, flushes angrily. The others go on up to their groups, but he lingers.

"Just don't concern yourself too much about the boys in my group, Mr. Bodkin," he says.

"I'm not. I just thought I'd let you know."

"The only con*spiracy* in this institution," he says, "is the one in which you yourself are engaged. The conspiracy of disinterest, Mr. Bodkin."

"All right. Look, I'm a little tired." I rise and start for the door, but he takes me by the arm. I think that perhaps he is pushing his luck a little with my temperament.

"You won't be staying on much longer, I trust," he says. "Where do you plan to go? Any prospects? I know a few people. I might be of assistance."

I take his hand out of the crook of my elbow. "Tell me something, Libby."

"What would you like me to tell you?"

I give him one of my most meaningful stares. "Just this: are you serious?"

"Yes," he says, his jaw quivering in a futile attempt to set it in an expression of defiance. "But you are not. And therein lies the difference between us."

"That's a good distinction," I say sincerely. "I like that."

"Thank you. I am therefore counting on never seeing you again after this morning. You have a conscience at least, and I'm sure that you can't help but recognize the truth of what I said to you last night. You even admitted it yourself."

"Yes, I did."

"Well then, the proper course of action follows logically: you'll have to leave. I can lend you a few dollars if you like."

"That's very kind of you."

"Not at all," he says, clasping his hands behind him and squaring his shoulders. "I have a genuine compassion for you. I think it truly a sorry state of affairs when the only people a man can find in this world to stand up and defend him are lunatics."

There is a ruckus upstairs on the third floor—Group Three.

Smitty, the Day on the second floor, in Nod's group, shouts down the staircase. "Hey, Libby, your group is going wild, man. Get up there and turn them off, will you?"

"I'll be right there," says Libby.

"I mean right now!" cries Smitty. "I got enough to handle with my own boys. I can't hear myself think, fella!"

Libby heaves a sigh. "Excuse me, Bodkin, I've got to get up there. Remember, if you need a few dollars, just let me know."

He starts up the stairs, and I call after him. "Don't forget what I told you before. Have a talk with your boys, okay? About Nod. Because it's important."

He stops halfway up the stairs and looks down at me angrily. "You're not going then after all, are you?"

"No, of course not. Are you out of your mind? Listen, that's not what's important right now, anyway. You've got to talk to those boys. They're in a state. I can feel it, d'you know? There's a chance that their little plot against Nod may be more than an idle threat. I had a peculiar feeling about them the whole night. They're quite capable of murder, you know."

The noise in Group Three rises, and Smitty appears at the head of the stairs on the second landing. "Goddamnit!" he says. "What the hell are you doing down there, fella?"

Libby turns around and starts up the stairs, his eyes cast down. "All right, all right, I'm coming!"

As he reaches the second landing, two of his boys come running down the stairs and he grabs them by the collars of their pajamas. They were just on their way into Smitty's group, obviously with intentions of stirring up a little early morning mischief. Smitty appears on the landing again, his eyes full of disgust.

"Now look," he says to Libby, who is having a bit of

difficulty hanging on to the two little boys. "You keep your lunatics up there where they belong this morning, or I am coming up there personally and whip some ass. Is that clear?"

"Let me go, you white mother-fucker," says one of the boys to Libby.

"Revolooooshun, revolooooshun!'" The cry issues from the third floor, along with laughter and other interesting audacities as more boys from Group Three start to come down the stairs.

Smitty utters a brief note of disgust. Libby is in a confusion and close to panic. As I start up the stairs to lend a hand, Weasel appears at my side; he has finished up in his own quarters and seems delighted with the opportunity to discharge some of the wrath he has left over from the night. Between the four of us—Weasel, Smitty, poor Libby and myself—we manage to put down the insurgent chaos and drive it back up to the third floor.

The boys jump into their beds and cower in the corners. Smitty returns to his own group downstairs, and Weasel whips off his belt and lets it play a tune here and there. But Libby cries out at him. "Stop that at once. This is *my* group, Mr. Weasel. And I will handle them in the manner in which I see fit! Stop it, I said!"

"I heard what you said." Weasel takes one more stroke at the boy in his grip and then releases him. "You said I was conscientious. Seventeen thousand marks on the tape. But that ain't nothing. You ought to see how many marks I got on these boys here—ha, ha, ha!"

"I'm sorry, but I don't find that amusing," says Libby. He takes Wimsy's hand in his own, as though he wants to comfort both himself and the boy. Wimsy is embarrassed but afraid to draw his hand away. "I didn't know this about you, Mr. Weasel," continues Libby. "But now that I do, I am going to speak to Mr. Doberman about it the first chance I get. And I am going to see to it that you are fired forthwith. Along with Mr. Bodkin."

Weasel laughs heartily.

"See that?" says Punzel, with new-found courage. He is in a lower bunk, and he gets up on his hands and knees and pokes his head out. "Mr. Libby is the best counselor in the whole world. He don't beat on us like the rest of them do here. He is going to get you fired, Mr. Weasel, yeah, yeah. He is going to get *ev*erybody who beats on us fired. He is the only one cares about us poor little boys. Right, men?"

"Yeah, yeah."

"That's right, Punzel."

"Hooray for Mr. Libby . . . hooray, hooray!"

"Shut up your mouths!" says Weasel.

They settle down.

Libby says, "I will not permit you to speak to these children in that fashion, Mr. Weasel. This is *my . . . my* group! I must ask you to leave at once."

"Don't you see what they are doing to you, man?" says Weasel, almost compassionately. "They *play*ing you. You don't fall for that 'hooray, hooray,' do you?"

"You heard our counselor," says Punzel, pointing his finger like a schoolteacher at Weasel. "He wants you to leave, yeah. Because you beat on us. You are a bad man. You . . . you are a big black faggit, ha, ha . . ."

"Hum?" Weasel's eyes grow large and round, and he stares at Punzel. Suddenly it is very quiet. Weasel takes one step toward the boy, who, obviously regretful of what he has just said, cowers back against the wall in terror.

"What's that you call me, boy?" says Weasel softly. He tilts his head and looks at Punzel out the corners of his eyes.

"Nothing, nothing . . ." says Punzel. "I didn't call you nothing, Mr. Weasel."

"Nothing?" says Weasel. "Good." He releases the boy from that frightening gaze and glances around at the others. "And I am glad that he said, 'Nothing.' Because for a minute there I thought that he said, '*Some*thing.' And then I would had to hurt him. And Mr. Weasel he don't like to hurt nobody lest he *have* to. Understand?" There is silence. He turns to Punzel. "Understand?"

"Yes, sir," says the boy hoarsely.

Libby, in whose eyes Punzel's terror has been reflected during that uneasy silence, is making a desperate attempt to get a grip on himself. His hands are shaking and he thrusts them quickly into his coat pockets. "I'm afraid I'll have to ask you to leave, Mr. Weasel."

"Leave?" says Weasel. His voice booms and his eyes twinkle. "Sure! I'm tired. I've been up all night, see? I don't *want* to be here right now. I just thought I would be friendly and help you out. But now I see you don't want me to help you out. So here's what I say: I say, 'Okay, Mr. Libby, you on your own.' The Weasel he don't come where he ain't wanted. Beside, you say you going to get me fired, right? So that's good. Now you don't have to worry no more about me. The Weasel ain't going to be around to bother you no more. Right?"

"Yes, I'm afraid that's true," says Libby, regaining his composure. "I am going to speak to Mr. Doberman first chance I get today. All the same . . . all the same, I hope there are no hard feelings between us—" He tries to smile and extends his hand; he wants Weasel to shake it.

"See what I told you, Bodkin?" cries Weasel in amazement. "This here man is a lunatic! From the word go . . . ha, ha, ha!" He takes me by the arm and steers me toward the door. "Come on, Jew, let us get some breakfast."

In the passageway we discover Nod pressed into the corner near the door. He has obviously been listening to us.

"You better get down to your group," I say. "Smitty is going to be angry with you."

"Please don't tell on me, Bodkin," he says. "I got to go in there and ask those boys something."

"Go ahead, boy!" says Weasel. "Me and Bodkin we have nothing to do with that group no more. The sun is up and you are on your own." He winks at me.

Nod looks at Weasel quizzically, shrugs his shoulders and walks into the room. Weasel and I stand at the door and watch.

"Mr. Libby?" says Nod. "I would like to ask your boys here something—"

Libby turns on him angrily. "What? Oh . . . it's you. What are you doing up here, Nod? Go on back to your own group. You can ask them some other time. We've got to get this place cleaned up before breakfast. We're running late. They're not even dressed."

"But it's very important, Mr. Libby."

"I said get back to your group—you'll speak to them later!" He is overwrought, is Libby. His boys, now that they think Weasel and I have gone, have started in again. The room is in disarray; clothes, blankets, towels, marbles, playing cards and other things are scattered over the floor.

"Quiet down!" cries Nod. "I got to ask you something."

"Not now, Nod," says Libby. "Come back later."

"Later is too late. Maybe I will be dead later," says Nod

with solemnity. He cups his hands around his mouth and shouts, "Shut up! I got to talk to you!"

"Okay, okay," says Punzel, signaling with one hand at the others to be quiet. "Quiet down, Killer here want to talk to us, ha, ha, ha . . ."

"Ha, ha, ha . . ."

"I ain't no killer," says Nod evenly, "and that's what I come to tell you."

There is a pause.

"Sure, sure," says Punzel. "Is that all you got to say?"

Nod is already dressed. He even has on his coat and galoshes and hat. He puts his hands in the back pockets of his trousers and glances around the room at the eleven boys in their pajamas. "Yes," he says.

He turns around and walks toward the door. There are tears in his eyes, and he doesn't seem to see Weasel or me.

"Don't worry about it, son," I say as he passes by us. "Nobody is going to hurt you. That's just a lot of talk."

Nod's eyes widen and his arm shoots forward, one finger pointing down the staircase. *"There* . . . there come the *real* killer! Evil, evil . . ."

Doberman is coming up the stairs with a brisk, brand-new executive stride, two steps at a time.

"Take this boy back to his quarters, Mr. Weasel," he says without pausing or looking at us. The order has that air of authority which knows it will be obeyed at once; it is very unlike Doberman. Weasel casts a contemptuous look at his back and then takes Nod downstairs.

"What is the meaning of this!" cries Doberman, plunging into the room. "Mr. Libby, why are these children still in their pajamas?"

Though they've seen Doberman enter, the boys take no

notice of him and continue to be disorderly. Libby is surprised and upset by Doberman's unexpected appearance,
and by now is so nervous that his nose has begun to bleed.
He dabs at it with his handkerchief. "Mr. Doberman, I . . .
it is difficult. Mr. Weasel, sir, has been interfering with my
business. He is brutal. He beat several of the boys with a
belt just a few minutes ago. And I must tell you . . . if I
can't have the cooperation of the staff, I can hardly be
expected to have the cooperation of the children. I'm sorry.
I didn't know this about Mr. Weasel . . . didn't know it last
night. But now that I do, I'd suggest, sir, that he also be
dismissed . . . along with Mr. Bodkin. Brutality and disinterest, those are the principal evils— Quiet down, all of
you! Don't you see that the Director is in the room? Quiet, I
said!"

"You heard your counselor, didn't you?" says Doberman. "Quiet down at once . . . Mr. Libby, I would like to
speak to them. Get them quiet." What does he want to talk
to them about? I wonder. He is looking very stern and
dapper this morning.

"Yes, sir, immediately," says Libby. "Listen here, all of
you—Punzel, put that pillow down . . . put it down! You
there, get off the window sill—you'll hurt yourself! Wimsy!
My God, what are you doing to Wimsy! Stop that at once!
What are you doing to him! All of you, quiet! Immediately!
I . . . I . . ."

Weasel appears at my side, puts his arm around my
shoulder and sticks his head in the door. "Now that is
something funny," he whispers with a broad grin.

"I know."

"Doberman is a dope."

"Do you think so?"

"Yes," he says. "But I don't like it."

"I know."

"They got to show respect for him. It ain't right."

He takes a few steps into the room, removes his belt, holds it up in the air behind Doberman's and Libby's backs and looks at the children fiercely. He also places a fore-finger over his lips. Within a minute the boys are quiet and sitting on their beds obediently.

"Now, that's much better," says Doberman. "Much better."

"You see?" says Libby, smiling nervously and trying to contain his astonishment. "They are beginning to respect me, sir. It has taken a few months to convince them that I really have their best interests at heart, but now that they are beginning to understand the fact . . . well, I should say that in just a few more weeks we'll have here the most well-behaved group in the whole place. Patience and perserver-ance, an enlightened approach—"

"Hey," says Wimsy in all innocence, "what you doing there, Mr. Weasel? I thought you be fired."

Doberman turns around, nonplused. Libby is also non-plused, but he is angry and humiliated as well. His Adam's apple bobs, his lips purse and the little muscles on the sides of his jaw twitch. There is also the tic in his right eye. His nose, however, has stopped bleeding.

I can't see Weasel's face, but at the back of his neck veins appear.

Doberman stammers something about the belt, but the only thing that comes across is his unhappiness. Everyone else remains quiet. We are tense; we are waiting for him to say something that we can understand. He says, "Mr. Weasel, please leave this room at once. I shall expect you in my office in exactly fifteen minutes. Good morning."

Weasel clenches his fists. His shoulders rise and he turns around and starts to walk out of the room. His head is thrust forward and down, defiantly, like a man who knows he is coming up against a stone wall and is determined to plunge through it.

"Bye-bye, you big black faggit," says Punzel. "I told you you was going to be fired, ha, ha—"

Weasel winces, but he keeps walking. He walks into the hall, doesn't look at me as he passes, and rushes down the stairs.

Laughter and insults from the boys cheer him on his way. Libby and Doberman try to bring order, but they cannot.

I go downstairs. Weasel is nowhere to be found. He is neither in the courtyard nor the mess hall. Perhaps he has gone up to Doberman's office.

I eat alone. The mess hall is full of noise. Trembley, Ashe and Boober beckon me to their table across the way. I wave at them and smile, and stay where I am. They shake their heads and laugh among themselves—at me and my solitudes. The eggs are delightfully greasy and I eat with good appetite.

The hall empties. I go to the urn and draw myself another cup of coffee. It is a metallic, rigorous drink, and it makes one suffer, but not so magnificently that I would feel right in bragging about it afterward. One chokes it down and thinks: A good penance. It will even make it more difficult to get to sleep this morning.

At last, into the empty mess hall comes Libby with his group. He has not been diligent in making sure that they dress themselves properly—he hasn't had time to, I suppose. I count three boys with their galoshes unbuckled, one without a hat, four without coats and six with dirty faces. He marches them to their table and then proceeds to the kitchen door and pounds on it. Now he will have to haggle with the cook to get food for his boys. The cook will not like this: late breakfast, extra work, disorder. The chief cook, Schmidt, is a pertinacious man. He drinks a lot. He is a German. When he is drunk, he likes to boast that he was a storm trooper. When he is sober, a sergeant in the United States Marine Corps. One doesn't know what to believe. It makes no difference. In both instances he plays himself up to be the most imaginative of men. He comes out of the door with a cleaver in his hand. He is sober but red in the face. He calls Libby many nasty names.

Libby is not in a conciliatory mood, and waxes indignant. Whereupon Schmidt calls him a Jew. Libby replies that he is a Presbyterian, but that he would be proud to be a Jew: "I do not consider that an insult." Then he calls Schmidt a bad cook and a drunkard, and even threatens to have him fired. Libby wants to have a lot of people fired. Schmidt's cleaver doesn't seem to put him off a bit—at least he doesn't show that it does.

In the end, Schmidt charges back into the kitchen and begins to shout at his helpers. He is obliged to serve Libby's boys. He knows this but likes to protest before doing so. That is the spice of life for Schmidt. Actually, at bottom, he is the mildest of men. He has been here five years and has never hurt anybody with his cleaver, except himself, when he chopped off the index finger of his left hand while attacking a side of pork.

Libby returns to his boys at the table. They are loud and unmannerly. He is worn out with too many execrations. He sits at the table. The boys are laughing and cursing and ringing the silverware. He is dazed. He looks now like a stone idol. At the drop of a hat—one feels sure of this—he will issue a wise platitude. His hair is messed up and matted. There are beads of sweat on his brow. He has removed his coat; part of his shirttail is sticking out of his dungarees. He sits quietly. Schmidt shouts in the kitchen. The boys carry on. But he, Libby, sits, he sits. I rise and head for the door. He sees me now. He didn't before. He flushes. But I smile at him and wave. He flashes me an angry look and then quickly turns on his boys and reprimands them for something in an unassailably admirable style.

About a month ago Libby and I had a chat, and at one moment I asked him why he didn't have a shot at hitting them, at least once anyway. "You don't have to beat them black and blue," I said. "Just a little cuff now and then, to let them in on something that's immediately comprehensible."

We were in my sitting room; he had just got off duty, and the children were asleep. We were on much better terms at the time. But he became agitated as soon as I broached the subject.

"I tried hitting them once," he replied. "Several weeks ago I slapped Punzel in the face. I was at my wit's end and was beginning to think that perhaps this was the only way to get the situation under control. But you see, Bodkin, I have studied, I'm educated, I have a knowledge of history. Do you understand? The boy's face is black. My hands are white. When I struck him, they looked even whiter. Believe me, that is the exact truth. At this point in history, it is a blasphemy for a white man to strike a black man. One immediately sees the black dead, in chains and humiliation, and they pass judgment on you. If you allow yourself to be imaginative for a moment, you even seem to hear a terrible cry out of the past, an impotent cry for vengeance. Any educated person who doesn't understand this is a fool. Bodkin, I will not strike any child in this institution ever again. And rest assured, I am a man of principle and will keep my word. Brutality is evil, and in the long run it is entirely ineffective. I must find some other method of dealing with the situation. In fact, I have already found one. Don't judge by appearances. Though my boys seem to be wild and out of hand, they really aren't. The truth of the matter is that at bottom I am having an excellent effect on their character."

RUNAWAYS

The staff house is quiet today. I run into no one in the lobby, on the stairs or along the passage which leads to my room, my wonderful little room. I shut the door, lie down on my bed without taking my coat or shoes off and look out the window. I have a view of the road, a piece of the woods and a wide field of snow. It is very pleasant.

I pass several hours in this dreamy fashion, until I see two runaways out on the road. I can't make out their faces; their collars are turned up and they are too far away. It is cold out. The snow lies in thick drifts everywhere, even on the roads. The snowplow hasn't been along yet. The runaways are making slow progress. One of them is reluctant to continue. The other boy punches him in the arm now and again and then drags him along by the hand for a few steps. Repeatedly the reluctant one breaks loose, begins to head back for the gate, is caught by his partner and dragged along another few steps.

I telephone the main office at the school. Doberman answers. "Who are they?" he says. "Can you tell?"

"No, but I'm pretty sure it's Blinken and Nod. You'd better send someone after them right away, sir."

"Bodkin," he says, "would you mind?"

"Mind what?"

"Five counselors called in sick this morning. We're running rather short of help."

"All right. I can't sleep anyway. Say, Mr. Doberman . . . about Weasel. What did you say to him this morning? Did he come to your office? You know, I really think you ought to reconsider and keep him on. In fact, he has a lot of good qualities."

I hear him breathing heavily in the receiver, but he doesn't say anything.

"Mr. Doberman?" I say.

He hangs up.

I don my blue woolen hat, button up my coat, wrap my neck in my luxurious red scarf and go downstairs. Who needs sleep? I lift my legs high. The snow is powdery and ample. These runaways are a sad pair, to be sure; they will never get anywhere at that rate. I cut across the field through drifts that are waist high sometimes. The steam pours out of my mouth. This is better than sleep—better than all things. What should I do in this life if there were no runaways? What would the runaways do if there were no Bodkins? D'you see? How perfectly orderly everything is when one looks at it in that light? I cut through the woods and come out ahead of my little runaways, so that I have them between me and what they are running from.

They haven't spotted me yet. "Don't be scared, Blink," says Nod. "We got to get on. Don't give me no more trouble now, okay? You will see. When we get to the city, everything is going to be fine."

He has Blinken by the arm again and is pulling at him, but Blinken is beyond persuasion. He hangs his head and looks at the ground with a sullenness and bewilderment and sadness which disallow him to go on. Resignation has nothing to do with it. It is typical of him. He is a quiet shy child, and unlike Nod, rarely gets into trouble. He is without mischief, rueful and thin, the younger of the two. He has a habit of not looking at you while you are speaking to him, but when you have finished he will lift his head and show you his eyes. They are vacant and bleak, like a courtroom at dawn. The judge and jury have not yet arrived; one is thankful for this and doesn't stare into them for too long at a stretch. He is giving Nod a very hard time, but Nod is remarkably patient and will not quit either until Blinken gives in—which doesn't seem likely—or until both of them perish out here on the road.

Nod looks up and spots me, then gives a tug at Blinken and whispers at him frantically, "Here comes Bodkin. Come on!"

Blinken takes a quick look at me and then stares at his galoshes.

"Come on, come on, we got to go," cries Nod, tears of frustration in his eyes, and he runs across the road backward without checking on the traffic. His arms motion imploringly and angrily at his friend.

Blinken will have none of it and keeps his eyes cast

down. He'll stay where he is. I let him be and run after
Nod, who takes off down the left side of the road against
the traffic. There are a lot of cars, and the road is slippery; I
don't want to frighten him lest he panic and run under
somebody's wheels.

He slips finally, falls into a drift on the shoulder and
clutches his ankle. He has given it a turn. I take him by the
wrist and the back of his collar, lift him to his feet and let
him have out with his blasphemies.

"Are you finished now?" I say after a bit.

"Yes."

"Sure you don't have anything else on your mind?"

"Nothing."

"Let's go, then."

He limps a little, theatrically, as I usher him back to his
friend, who is awaiting our return.

"Why didn't you *run,* Blink?" says Nod, slapping his
forehead by way of a greeting. "Between you and Bodkin
here I am never about to get *no*where in this world."

Blinken gives him a sad look and shrugs his shoulders.

Nod laughs woefully and pats his friend on the back.
"Okay now," he says, "come on, we are going back. Now
we don't have to miss no meals today. Hey! What's the
*ma*tter with you, boy? You are sad when we run away, and
you are sad when we run back. In fact, you are so sad,
Blinkers, you funny!"

A sorrowful laugh issues from Blinken's lips, and Nod,
contenting himself with this as a sign that his friend is still
alive inside, turns to me. "Okay, Bodkin, we are ready.
Let's go."

We start back. I walk between them with my hands on
their shoulders, and by and by Nod tells me all about it,
gesturing excitedly and looking straight ahead. "See, about

two weeks ago, me and Blinken we took the Page in the
closet with us. And Page he let up a holler, I tell you, to
beat the band. So we let him go right away. But then he
went and got his boys together from upstairs, and they
come down and beat on us a trifle. That was right after
lunch, during the rest period. And that faggit was on their
group up there. That Libby. He can't handle them maniacs,
I can tell you for sure."

"That's not entirely true, Nod," I say. "He's a very nice
man, Mr. Libby is."

"Sure, sure. Anyway, they come down the stairs like a
herd of elephants. It like to break your ears in two. The
whole group. They call us names and beat on us a trifle.
And that's okay. It isn't the first time, I think to myself, and
it isn't the last."

"Where was your counselor all of this time?"

"Smitty? He was down in the athletic office, getting us
some checkerboards, see?"

"Sure."

"Anyway, me and Blinken, we forget all about it. Because we don't look for trouble with nobody. But now they
say we kill the Page because of how they beat on us. Tell
me something, Bodkin. Is there anybody so crazy as to
think that the Blinken and me is going to kill the poor little
Page just because he holler in the closet and got some
boys together to beat on us a trifle—?"

"I suppose there is."

He laughs softly and thrusts his hands in his coat pockets. "You are right. There is."

He is silent for a minute, and then he bursts out again. "I
mean, you know, they had no *cause* to beat on us in the *first*
place. Because the poor little Page, he came down *ask*ing
for it. We did not force him into the closet. Some people

around here are like that. But me and Blinken? No, sir. So now they say they are going to kill us. To get even. *Even!* So I say to them yesterday, I say, 'Even? Well, maybe you will get even with Steven, you faggits, but I tell you, you are just getting odd with Nod, and if anybody lay one finger on me or the Blinkers here, somebody is going to be odd with God and my brother *too,* and they will be a bloody nose everyplace and you bet on it.' They make a boy sick. They are looking very hard for an excuse to cut me up—or anybody up. That is going on a long time with them. That big one up there, *Pun*zel. He come out from a talk with his social worker this morning and he say to me, 'Listen here, nigger. I know why you sit in that snow. Guilt *feel*ings.' So I say, 'What do you mean by that, Pumpernickel?' And he say, 'It mean that you done a bad thing, that you kill the Page. And then you feel so bad, you got so much guilt *feel*ing, that you got to go sit down in the snow and hurt your little buns there with the ice-cold, so that your inside feel better.' 'So how come my inside don't feel better?' I say. 'Because your inside be black,' he say. 'So what do that make me if my inside black?' I say. And he say, 'It make you a sadomasochist,' and he walks away. So I call after him, 'You motherfucker.' And then he turn around and give me a look and say, 'You dead, little boy. I kill you tonight. Because you kill the Page.' And then he laugh and look at me in such a way as I know he means it. And then he tells the same to Blinken . . . I got to go to the bathroom . . . oh, Mr. Bodkin, so bad. Excuse me."

He walks off the shoulder to the edge of the woods and relieves himself at the foot of a tree, with his back to the road and his head bowed.

To pass the time while we're waiting, I ask Blinken what

his opinion of the situation is, but he merely shrugs.

"Well . . . do you think you ought maybe try to explain things to those boys in Group Three, Blinken?"

He looks up at me. "No," he says. He has an even, deeply serious voice and measures his words carefully. "They are crazy, Mr. Bodkin. Nod he sit down in the snow for all of us boys here. And he like to freeze to death. Then they say he kill the Page. Right?"

"Right . . ."

"So what do you expect to *splain* to such a bunch of boys as that? You splain your brain off and they don't care one little bit. Anyway, they are not killing nobody. They are just a lot of talk. They are just liars—"

"Blinken," says Nod, pulling up his zipper as he walks back to us, "you got one fault. You think everybody is a liar."

Blinken is startled; he wasn't aware that Nod could hear him. He looks at the ground, embarrassed. "No I don't," he mumbles.

"Yes you do," says Nod with a big grin, putting his arm around his friend's shoulder. "And that is bad. You got to have more be*lief* in people when they talk to you. They are no liars. They aim to kill you and me both. They are telling the George Washington truth, and you better know it."

I put my hands on their shoulders, and the three of us start to walk again. "Why, Bodkin," says Nod, "Blinken here, he does never believe even me, who is his best friend. About anything! Doberman kill the Page, I told him, and I told everybody else too. But they don't believe the old Nod. After the riot is over and I go sit down in the snow for all them skinny little ungrateful boys and like to freeze to death, I tell them *still:* 'Doberman kill the Page.' But do they listen to Nod? No, Blinken and all the rest of them, they listen to all the big white liars in here, and to that fairy Weasel, because he say he is going to write letters to their mamas. They don't even *have* mamas, most of them. They are crazy, all right . . . Well, 'that is life,' like my brother say. Right, Bodkin?"

"Sure, son."

"You know," he says with the air of having just reached an important decision, "I don't like how you say, 'son,' Bodkin. Don't call me that no more."

We are silent for a minute. "All right," I say. "But look, there are a couple of things you're off base about. First of all, about Mr. Doberman. The autopsy came in last night, and it said that Page died of a heart attack."

"Sure, sure, I know," Nod says sardonically. "They told us all about that autopsy jive and the heart attack this morning. And everbody be*lieves* it too! Oh boy."

"Well? And they believe it because . . . because it's true, Nod. And that means that neither Mr. Doberman nor anybody else killed Page—it means he just died. So forget about it. And second of all, Blinken is right. Nobody is going to be killing anybody around here. I'll speak to the Days on Group Three and have them get everything straightened out between you two and Punzel and the rest of them. So you just rest easy, all right?"

"The Days?" he says. "That's real fine. But I tell you something, you better talk to the night *watch*man too. His name is Mr. Jewish Bodkin. Because those little liars in Group Three? They say they are going to kill us in our sleeps."

"Oh?"

"That's right, Bodkin. In our *sleeps*. And I can't keep my

eyes open twenty-four hours, can I? And I tell you something: that gives me no comfort. Because the other night, you know? When Doberman kill the Page? Where were you? *I* know. *I* know where. You were down there in the sitting room, Body, fast asleep. No, sir, no comfort at all."

"Listen here. First of all, I wasn't asleep."

"Well, maybe you know about that better than I do."

"Maybe I do. And second of all, Mr. Doberman did *not* kill Page. I just told you. The autopsy . . . it was a heart attack. Page died. He just died."

Nod tilts his head, looks up at me out of the corner of one eye, a studied theatrical look with a mocking half-smile, and then looks up at the sky as though there were some phantom there, with whom he exchanges a knowing glance. He shrugs his shoulders, and we don't talk much more until we return to the courtyard.

As soon as we arrive, I hear Doberman's voice. Where is he? I hear it echo and bounce all over the buildings. One minute I think he is at my heels, and the next minute in the sky. There he is, up in his office, leaning out the window and waving his arm. "Bring them up here, Bodkin," he calls. "I want a word with them."

Nod clutches my arm. "Please, Body," he says hoarsely; he is frightened. "Don't take us up there. Take us back to the group."

But there is nothing for it. I drag them up to Doberman's office. Blinken is no trouble and comes along quietly, but Nod trembles all over and gags on his own protestations. It is not healthy, doing this to the boy. I don't like it, but I do it all the same. Doberman calls; I do it. One can't play pigeon to fears and phantoms; it slows everything down.

Doberman is writing anxiously on one of his little note-pads when we enter. He stops at once and slips it into the top drawer of his desk. He flushes when he greets us.

On my way out, while passing through the courtyard, I notice that there is a little white button pinned on the front of everyone's jacket, inmates and staff alike. The buttons, fastened with safety pins, are made of white cardboard, and there is writing on them. But the writing is small and crowded, so that you have to squint and get very close to read it. It says, "Let's try to change things for the better so that James Page will not have died in vain."

According to Ernest Brown, one of the Days, the buttons were Doberman's idea. He had the office girls working feverishly the whole morning, cutting out the cardboard in circles and writing the slogan on them. The buttons were distributed about a half-hour ago, and apparently everyone is required to wear them for a week. Which isn't likely to happen, because already most of the buttons are wet from the snow and have begun to shred and fall apart.

In fact, it's curious altogether. What can be going through Doberman's mind? ". . . so that James Page will not have died in vain"—what does that mean? That's the sort of thing one says about a martyr or a soldier—so that the living will carry on the cause he died for. And even then it's ludicrous. Why should one carry on another man's cause? And doesn't everyone die "in vain"? Of course, if we have to entertain ourselves with soldiers and martyrs, then after they get their portion we must say, "Let's see to it that they did not die in vain." Because if we didn't, the enlist-ment of new soldiers and martyrs would become increas-

ingly difficult, and then how would we entertain ourselves?
But what has Page to do with this? He wasn't a soldier or a
martyr; in fact, he was perennially skeptical. How do you
attach a slogan like that to his death?

He's a puzzle, Doberman is. It is like that speech of his
last night about the packets of seeds. Why does he imagine
that everyone ought to feel responsible for Page's death?
What had anyone else to do with it? The boy simply died,
didn't he? "Of his own stink." Mischief or no mischief, bad
taste or no bad taste, there was something in that; even
though Doberman felt he had to apologize for it, there was
something in it, all the same. It may even have been the
most honest moment of his career.

However, if Doberman did in fact kill James Page, as
Nod so passionately believes, then everything fits. Then
Doberman would have to say, "Let's try to change things
for the better so that James Page will not have died in
vain." But if Doberman did not kill Page, then one has a
puzzle. I think one has a puzzle; Doberman wouldn't hurt a
fly.

What is even more curious is that no one, neither the
staff nor the inmates, seems to think this button business in
the least out of the way. They take it as a matter of course.
So used have they become to Doberman's rhetorical fancies,
I suppose, that these buttons are seen to be quite ordinary.

I return to the staff house and toss and turn in bed with
my clothes on for a couple of hours, but I can't drop off
properly and finally go downstairs. Weasel, Boober, Trembley and Ashe are playing poker in the lobby. Okay.

"Deal me in."

They can't sleep either. Who sleeps? Nobody sleeps.

Whoever says he sleeps lies. Five players makes a good contest. We play for pennies, a blood game. What's that? Full house, Weasel? No good. "Four Kings," I say.

"Four Kings!" says Weasel. "Who deal this carnival?"

"I did," says Ashe.

"Oh sure. Every hand a miracle when the Ashes here put down the cards. Give me that deck, nigger."

So Ashe gives it to him, and the game takes a decided turn for the grim. Weasel shuffles with malice. He deals just what we deserve, himself included. He is in the hole and has to touch Ashe for a dollar.

Weasel has been fired, and this hasn't done anything in the way of sweetening his humor. He has already told the other three all about it. Their sympathies have turned. He has been the target of so many of their complaints for so long, and now, all of a sudden, he is the sacrificial goat. They pour out libations: alcoholic, verbal and lachrymal. I would howl if I weren't so beat. Doberman gave Weasel a week's notice; he hasn't a cent, Weasel, and so will have to curb his appetite for the grand and vengeful gesture and eat his notice instead. Doberman ought to have given him a little bonus and sent him packing. Keeping him around in this kind of a mood is like letting a mad dog hang around the nursery. Doberman is not wise, not wise. He shouldn't have fired Weasel in the first place.

Here comes bad news in person, Hanover Jones.

"Telephone call for you, Bodkin," he says. "It's Nod."

Nod? How did he get to a telephone? My four buddies look at me. I hurry up out into the hall and grab up the receiver. "Hello?"

"Bodkin?" whispers Nod.

"Yes?"

"This is Nod."

"Where are you, son?"

"In Doberman's office. Don't talk. Just listen."

"Okay."

He's whispering, a note of panic in his voice. "I got a . . . I found a confession up here. It was written by Doberman. He killed the Page, all right. It says right here . . . listen to this: 'I killed James Page.' That's what it says. It goes on like that for a lot of pages. It is all handmade in ink. And he signed it too. I got it right here. I'm scared, Body. I'm alone. Doberman he sent Blinken back to the group and kept me here. You got to help me. Doberman he be coming right back any minute—"

"Where did he go?"

"To get me some ice cream. Or that's what he said. But I ain't eating it."

"Listen—"

"Maybe he will poison it, like he done Page. Body, I am so scared! I *knew* I was going to find something outstanding up here. Soon as he shut the door, I start to look through his drawers, and that was the first thing I find. Right there on top, in the biggest drawer in the desk. Like as if he *want*ed somebody to find it. How come he left me alone with that notepad in that drawer like that? I'm scared, Body. I don't know what to do. I almost cry out the window, but then I think: No, can't do that. Nobody will believe me, see? They say, 'Oh, that crazy boy again.' And then Doberman he will be in here in a flash. And burn up the paper. And kill me sure as shooting. It is lucky I see these numbers here. I prayed to God that you would be at the staff house. Doberman got the numbers taped right onto the telephone. Real neat. Staff house. Right here. He thinks

of everything, all right. Oh God, help me. He will do me out
of the world just like that. Neat. Like the numbers. He got
everything taped. And I begged him to keep Blinken here.
But he send him back to the group alone. Alone! And those
boys up there, they are going to kill Blinken. You bet on it.
Because now he don't have me to protect him. Doberman
he has it all figured out. Himself will take care of me, and
he will let Punzel and them maniacs take care of Blinken.
How come he want to do us like that? What did we ever do
to him? Hurry, Bodkin. Please come and help me. Please,
please. If you do, I won't even say I got a brother any more.
I promise. Because I don't. I don't have a brother. I only
got you, Bodkin. You are the only nice man in this whole
place." He breaks into sobs.

"Listen," I say. "Nod? Listen to me. Try and get a grip
on yourself, son. It's probably just a misunderstanding, that
note. He doesn't really mean it, probably. That writing, it's
just writing—see? It's not something that's supposed to be
taken seriously. Mr. Doberman is always making jokes. A
sort of joke, do you see?"

"No!" he cries. "It's no joke! Please, Body! You got to
believe me! I swear to God! I didn't make it up! I got it
right here . . . you got to come quick. Oh Lord, here he
come up the stairs. I hear him. Please, Bodkin. You got to
hurry. I can't even scream for help. Nobody listens to a
screaming boy in this place. They just say, 'Oh, another
screaming boy.' Please, God . . . Bodkin, help me. I got to
hang up."

"All right, listen to me. Stuff the notepad inside your
shirt. Don't say anything to Mr. Doberman about it. I'm
coming right over."

"Okay, thanks, thanks," he whispers. He hangs up.

I return to the table and tell everybody that Nod was just playing around with one of the telephones in the athletic office.

"I'm going for a walk," I say. "See you later." I scoop up my pile of pennies and leave. They grumble a bit and throw a few unpleasant remarks at my back. I was ahead of the game. People don't like you to quit when you're ahead of the game. I know why well enough. Their grumbling is good-natured though.

I hurry through the woods, walking a hundred steps, running a hundred steps, a Boy Scout trick. I was never a member myself, but I'm not pleased that I missed out on it, no matter what people say. The Boy Scouts have a special wisdom. I know; many is the night I've pored over their handbook. It is an esoteric literature, not for everyone, and in it are secrets which are both useful and mysterious.

It is about a quarter to six when I arrive in the courtyard; the fog is blowing over the trees and rooftops, and the wind is coming up strongly; a dark, bitter night. The lights are on in all three wings of the building, those dull yellowish lights that cast no beams through the windows. Only a faint glow hangs over the yard.

Not a soul stirs in any of the wings. Everybody is in the mess hall. The tinkle of the silver in the distance sounds like bells from another, gayer world. From out here even the laughter and shouts seem to be coming from a high and fancy place. It is all muffled and changed by the walls, by the night, by the distance . . . I like passing through the empty yard and listening to them in the mess hall down the way. It gives one intimations; for a moment one thinks that surely if the proper place could be found for those voices in the night, they might become just what they seem to be from here—and maybe they are already! Maybe if I were to walk into the mess hall this minute, I would discover them in the robes of kings, decked out in silver and gold embroideries, rubies on their crowns. There would be singing and dancing, lutes and harps and tambourines—and bowls of oranges, apples, guavas from the warm countries and purple grapes . . . and divine dialectic passing like an angel among the company. And there would be lovely maidens . . . there really ought to be girls here. Why are there no girls? The whole place is a penance, don't make any mistake about it.

I find Doberman alone in his office, looking very unhappy. We make small talk for a while, and then I ask, "Where's Nod?"

"I sent him on to eat his supper, of course. Why do you ask?"

"Oh . . . just wondering."

"You know, Bodkin," he says, resting his elbows on the desk and rubbing his eyes with the palms of his hands, "that boy has upset me considerably—"

"Oh?"

"He had a tantrum right after you left. Accused me of killing Page. Right to my face. It was even worse than the other night."

"Oh?"

"Yes *Oh!*" he says angrily, slapping the desk. His eyes are red. "Is that all you can say, Bodkin? *Oh? Oh?*"

"I'm sorry, sir—"

He is ashamed of himself at once, and begins to pout. "Never mind, never mind . . . I lost my temper. The boy . . . he's upset me . . ."

"I understand, sir."

RUNAWAYS

"Those are terrible accusations . . ."

"I understand—"

"What do you understand, Bodkin?" he snaps. "You understand nothing! Do you think that those accusations of his are *new* to me? Well, they are not. I have heard them before. There is a creature in my head. He makes the same accusations. He makes them night and day. It is all I can do to keep my sanity."

"I know. It's difficult, sir."

"Difficult?" he cries. "It's impossible! And the boy only compounds the problem. And the horror of it is, Bodkin, that the boy does not understand the *real* nature of my guilt. He does not understand the full ex*tent* of it. And that, finally, is what exasperates me and brings me to the point of tears: the injustice that is perpetrated on me by his misunderstanding of the *real* nature of my guilt and the full ex*tent* of it. He does not do justice to my evil. My evil is much greater than he would have it. Much larger! But how can I tell him this, Bodkin? How can I tell him! Much . . . much larger!" He puts his face in his hands again and begins to weep.

"See you later, sir," I say. "Hope you start feeling better."

In the mess hall the noise turns your stomach; the food doesn't look too good, either. Beef stew, and nobody is touching it. They are eating the bread, mainly. Nod lights up and waves at me from the other side, and I go over to him.

"How do you feel?" I whisper. "I came as quick as I could. Do you have the confession?"

"Yes." He pats his shirt front, and I hear the crackle of paper. He looks about him nervously at the other boys in

[173]

the group, who are sitting around the circular table, staring at us and whispering. Smitty, the counselor, looks at me with a touch of hostility, but I smile at him in my most disarming fashion.

"Have you shown it to anyone yet?" I whisper.

"You crazy, Bodkin? No."

"Not even to Blinken?"

"Sure, I showed it to him. But he can't read and he don't believe."

"Well," I say, "you better let me have it, son. I'll take care of it."

"Not here," he says, looking at me distrustfully. "Later. After the movie."

"Is there another movie tonight? Christ."

"Yeah. I will come down to the sitting room after Smitty leaves."

"Okay. Just promise me one thing."

"Sure."

"Don't show it to anybody until I've seen it, okay? Promise?"

"Yes."

"At any rate," I say, smiling at him with as much condescension as I can muster, "Doberman didn't try to kill you this afternoon, did he."

He looks up and narrows his eyes at me. "I don't know if he tried or not," he says sharply. "I didn't eat that ice cream."

"Something wrong, Bodkin?" says Smitty, a note of displeasure in his voice.

It is a touchy situation here. Every counselor has such a delicate time keeping the balance that any outsider is immediately regarded as a dangerous intruder who may upset the works.

"Nothing's wrong, Smitty," I say. "Nod and I we had a bet on the football game this afternoon, and I just came over to pay up."

"What football game was that?" Smitty says.

I don't know. I don't even know the names of any football teams. "The Monkeys and the Dragons," I say. "Local outfits."

"Never heard of them. Who won?"

"The Monkeys won," says Nod defiantly. "That's who."

The boy is a dreamer, unmistakably a dreamer.

I fork over ten pennies, the whole of my poker winnings, to make it look authentic. He smiles at me, and then the other boys in the group, green with envy, start imploring me to bet with them too. On anything. Gamblers, all of them.

Smitty pounds his fist on the table and they quiet down. He says, "The boys aren't supposed to have money, Bodkin. They aren't supposed to be gambling neither."

Now I've put my foot in it, all right. I have to learn to be more diplomatic in situations like this. "That's absolutely right, Smitty," I say, and then, turning to the boys, "And don't you forget it. You listen to your counselor, d'you hear? Gambling is immoral . . . in fact, it's not even nice. And d'you know *why* I came here to pay up my bet with Nod? To teach you all a lesson. Right. And what was the lesson? 'Don't cross your bridges until they hatch out of the early bird.' There's a bit of financial wisdom for you. You think about it awhile, and maybe after you grow up a little you'll say, 'That Mr. Bodkin, he was really right about gambling.' Go ahead, you can laugh all you want to—just wait, you'll see . . . Bye, Smitty."

LADDERS AND
VISIONS

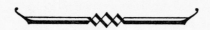

As I'm walking up the little cement walk that leads away from the mess hall, Pincher runs across the courtyard, waving his arms wildly. "Bodkin! Just the person I'm looking for! I was just coming to look for you!"

Wonderful.

"It's Miss Rose!" he cries. "You've got to come at once —at once, at once . . ."

I let him take me by the arm to the infirmary. He explains everything on the way, rapidly and excitedly, the steam sputtering out of his mouth.

It seems that Doberman assigned poor Pincher the task of informing Miss Rose of her retirement, of presenting her with the bonus check and of seeing to it that she remove herself. She is to be taken to a hotel in town. There she may remain for two weeks with all expenses paid, during which time she is to collect her thoughts and decide on her next move. It is well known that she has put away some money over the years; she has more than enough to live on for the remainder of her life. With the two-thousand-dollar bonus into the bargain there ought to be no concern over her. She is well heeled and quite crazy enough to get along splendidly in this world.

But she is a mule, alas, and that's difficult. Pincher paid her a visit at noon today and—"with the utmost in tact and cordiality, Bodkin!"—informed her that she had to get out right away because she had been replaced. Whereupon she grabbed the bonus check from him, tore it up in high style before his eyes and slammed the door in his face before he had enough presence of mind to put his foot in. She then bolted it. It is a heavy iron door. She refuses to leave, or to admit anyone, or to let anyone out. There are six boys in the infirmary.

Doberman gave instructions to let her alone until this evening; he thought it might be unsettling to the inmates, as well as the staff, to witness the forceful extrication of poor old noisy Miss Rose. And that, clearly, is what is going to be necessary: she will have to be removed by force.

It is Pincher's desire, however, that I first make an attempt at persuading her to give up the fort peacefully. "She likes you, Bodkin. She respects you. You know how to talk to her. She may listen to you. Please, Bodkin, you must at least *try*—it is absolutely essential!"

Pincher is also concerned about the six little boys who are in there with her. He has tried to get them to cooperate with him and open the door, but they don't answer; in fact, they have been very quiet all day, which is unlike them. He has heard them laughing softly on occasion, and off and on there have been soft ecstatic moans and sighs. *"God* knows what she's been doing to them in there! What could she be doing to them, Bodkin?"

"Beats me. But it sounds like fun, don't you think?" When he gives me a horrified look I wink at him, and he laughs in relief. One has always to wink at Pincher, to give him some visible sign of what's what. He laughs heartily, even. I like to see Pincher laugh. It makes me hopeful.

I have an hour or so to try out my persuasive talents. The boys will be kept in the mess hall after supper and shown a movie. If I fail to get her to come out by the time the movie is over, then I'm to quit, and after the boys have been put to sleep, Pincher will call the police and let them do the job. Apparently they are equipped to handle this sort of nuisance, though I should think that the fire department might be better.

We go up the narrow stairway to the vestibule adjacent to the infirmary. What's this? Sweetness and light: Miss Rose's replacement.

Pincher introduces me at once, the one benevolent gesture he has made me in our entire wretched acquaintanceship. "Miss Fein—Mr. Bodkin."

I'm so pleased—so very pleased to meet her. I express my pleasure without delay. She is lovely. She sits on a straight-back wooden chair, her legs crossed, and doesn't

rise when she shakes my hand. But she smiles, leans forward and touches her knee. She is my age. She has been
waiting here since noon. If only I had known! Waiting in
this dimly lit vestibule all by herself— what a waste! Her
hair is black. It touches her shoulders almost. She is built,
and has a lascivious gleam in her eye; it is gracefully in-
decent—a wordly woman who knows what she is about.
She is a Jew from Georgia. Her voice is nasal, and she has a
thick Atlanta drawl which is repulsive to me, but there are
compensations, infinite compensations . . . life is looking
up. I'll put cotton in my ears; what do I care about voices?
Here at last is something substantially interesting. The principal thing now is to get Miss Rose out of the infirmary. "It
is absolutely essential!" Pincher was right, no mistake about
it.

I put my mouth close to the iron door. "Miss Rose?" I
say. "It's me—Bodkin. Are you there? Can you hear me?
I'd like to speak to you for a minute."

But she makes no answer. I try again and turn on the
charm. Certainly she can hear me. I raise my voice and
implore her. But it's no use; she won't answer. A quarter of
an hour passes like this, and at last I turn back to Pincher
and shrug my shoulders. What is to be done?

Suddenly Pincher lights up. He has an idea. "The ladders
—I'll get ladders . . . perhaps the windows are unlocked."

"Probably not," I say.

"Yes, you're right," he says. "But at least we may get a
glimpse of what is going on up there. Why didn't I think of
this before! Wait right here. I'll go down and get Handy to
help me with the ladders from the basement."

Excellent. He hurries down the stairs and leaves me
alone with Miss Fein. There's an excitement straightway

swimming back and forth like a school of fish between the
two of us. I reach out one hand and stroke the side of her
face gently. She turns her lips into my palm and touches it
on the life line, just barely but precisely, with the tip of her
tongue. She looks up at me winsomely out of the corner of
her eye and smiles. My thumb glides around the rim of her
ear. She rises up out of her chair, slowly but with purpose,
and takes my shoulders in her fingertips. She closes her
eyes, tilts her head to the side, her face reaching for mine,
and we kiss and press against one another and touch one
another in many places. It is a remarkable situation, the
kind of gratuity one banks on in this life.

We separate as soon as we hear the door at the foot of
the stairs open. "Hurry, Bodkin," calls Pincher breathlessly.
"We have the ladders."

Down the stairs! Into the cold! Ladders? What ladders?
Silence!

Hanover Jones and Pincher have already set the two ladders side by side under the second-story window. Pincher
assures me that they are secure and sends me up at once,
calling his "essentials" and various encouragements and
flatteries after me.

Why am I going up a ladder in zero weather? So that I
can look into the infirmary and investigate the sick—I
ascend with alacrity. I make believe that I am engaged upon
the enterprise of eloping with Miss Fein—that here I am,
making my way up the rungs one by one, braving frostbite
barehanded, in order to rescue her from her wicked step-
father who beats her with chains. My coach-and-four waits
in readiness just around the corner, and soon, soon we shall
be away from all this, Miss Fein and I. We shall fly across
the expanse of the country—faster, faster!—in a single

night. We shall breakfast in my palace, my stately palace. It looks over the Pacific. One hears the dull roar of the ocean the day long—the great ocean that lies hundreds of feet below us. We shall have nothing but love and idleness, and elegant conversation and music, excellent company, the most digestible of foods, forever and ever—save in October. In October we shall be studious, for it is then that the gray whales sail by on their annual migrations, and we must observe them. We shall sit, then, hand in hand, in the observation tower and look very carefully into the deep and count attentively the great monsters as they roll by . . . because one must have some kind of important business— at least one month a year, I think—or else one might grow tired of his palace, his love and idleness, his music, his elegant conversation.

I reach the top of the ladder, and here is Miss Rose, looking through the window. She looks at me and smiles; she has been expecting me, it would seem. She is calm. Calm! She is composed. She has a poise, a quietude that I have never seen in her before. She gives me the willies. A little enigmatic smile plays about her lips. There is a touch of the sinister in that smile, as though she has a secret in her that is not quite on the up and up—some evil secret, in fact, which will allow her to be among people now and endure them. What that secret might be I don't know. I have an idea though. I'm not sure I like it much.

The window is locked, and I ask her to open up. "Just a little bit?" But she shakes her head and continues to smile.

Behind her, sitting on the floor, slouched back against the far wall, are her six little patients. They don't seem much interested in my appearance at the window. They have the same smile—Miss Rose's. Their eyes are glassy. The expression in them is one of lethargy, amusement and imperturbability. If I weren't so well acquainted with their habits and histories I might almost be persuaded that they know something worth knowing. They sit in an everlasting swoon, nodding their heads occasionally.

"Do you see anything, Bodkin?" calls Pincher from below.

"Yes."

He hurries up the other ladder, which is next to mine, and is horrified immediately. Looking through the window, he gasps like a woman and covers his gaping mouth with one hand. "Miss Rose!" he cries. "What have you done! My God, my God! Open the door for us—at once, at once—!"

But she remains unmoved and continues to smile as before. He gesticulates madly with his arms, so much so that I'm afraid he may upset both our ladders. I pat him on the back and exhort him to get a grip on himself.

"But, Bodkin!" he says. "Do you see? Can you imagine? She has drugged them! She has given them *che-mi-cals!* And herself too! Look at her! Ah God, Miss Rose, let us in . . . at once! I beg you, my dear, you don't know what you're doing . . . you'll kill yourself—and all of these boys as well. They're in a weakened condition *as* it is, my dear. They must be taken to a hospital at once, at once! I suspected that's what she was up to, Bodkin. Always fussing about with her tubes and whatnots. That is to say, I smelled it. I've been smelling the vile fumes all day, you know; I was simply afraid to admit it to myself. But it was there, I tell you, in the back of my mind—drugs! What shall we do, what shall we do?"

He throws up his arms, and I have quickly to push my

hand against the small of his back to keep him and his ladder from swaying. The wind is coming up harder out of the northeast.

Miss Rose bends over the little table at her side and writes something methodically with a fountain pen on a notepad. Then she holds it up to the window for me to see, and gazes into my eyes as I read. It says: "I saw you through the keyhole, Bodkin."

"What does she mean by that, Bodkin?" whispers Pincher, his chin almost touching my shoulder as he leans sideways to read the note. The steam out of his mouth drifts before my eyes.

"I don't know," I say.

Once again she bends over the table and writes, and once again holds up the notepad for me to read. It says: "I saw you caress her. Why did you never caress me?"

Which bewilders Pincher for a moment, and then he breaks into a broad grin.

"You and Miss Fein, eh, Bodkin?" he says, winking at me, and he nudges me in the ribs with his elbow. "Sly . . . sly—" But he nudges me a little too enthusiastically and I and my ladder go sliding away from him. I manage to stop myself, however, by pressing my hands firmly against the wall. I am at a precarious angle. Holding my breath, I clench my teeth and push myself back to a vertical position.

Pincher begins to apologize effusively. "Never mind," I tell him, "just try to calm yourself."

However, his thoughts are already elsewhere. His pragmatic humor has come back to him with inevitable grace, like a faithful pigeon. He snaps his fingers and hurries down the ladder about five rungs, so that he is below the window sill and out of Miss Rose's sight, and tugs at the legs of my

trousers and beckons me. I raise a forefinger apologetically
before Miss Rose, to indicate that I will return in a moment, and I go down to Pincher.

He is aflutter. He puts his head close to mine conspira-
torially; he has a plan. We are to play on Miss Rose's
sudden fit of romance. We are to turn it to our own advantage. "We can manipulate her now like a marionette," he
says. "She has shown us at last what her desires are. The
desires are the strings."

"Oh?" I say. "And what, Pincher, does she desire?"

"You! Ace Bodkin! She desires *you,* Bodkin!"

He whispers instructions and though I don't like the idea,
I see there is method in it all the same, that it is absolutely
imperative, in fact, that I go through with it—for the sake
of order, perhaps.

I ascend the ladder and confront the window, with
Pincher laughing into my shoes. "Miss Rose," I say, shouting so she can hear me through the glass. My voice bounces
all over the courtyard and comes back to me as if it were
someone else whispering in my ear, whispering shameful
things. "Miss Rose, I love you, my dear." I spread my arms
grandly. "Come, let us leave this madhouse. Let us fly away
to the warm countries. By the sea."

I pause to see how she interprets me so far. We stare at
one another for a while.

She takes to her notepad. "What about Miss Fein?" she
writes.

What about Miss Fein indeed.

"She is nothing to me," I say. "She offends me. She bores
me. She is vulgar and lewd. I confess that I did have a brief
moment with her in the vestibule, but it was she who se-
duced *me.* I succumbed to her, my dear, merely out of
pity—she is nothing to me, nothing!"

"But I am old," she writes. "It is late."

"But it's not! Not late at all! There is a whole life yet to live, Miss Rose. We shall go away together, you and I. I shall be your conquistador, your own personal Ponce de León. I shall lead you straight to the Fountain of Youth . . . the sweet, the scented waters . . . your limbs will turn supple, your skin smooth, your hair silky, your teeth will have a renascence."

A tear slides out of the inside corner of her left eye. I wish I too could weep. How human that would be. But it is too cold out here.

"What about money?" she writes.

Money, alas.

"I've some put by," I say. "Quite a treasure trove, as a matter of fact. And together with your bonus, why, we could live out our days like a king and a queen, never do another stitch of work, surround ourselves with pleasantries. What d'you say? Yes? Please say it. Give me a sign, and I'll be at the door in a moment. Come, a little sign, Miss Rose. Will you open your door for me?"

She shuts her eyes, inhales deeply through her nose and nods her head.

"Wonderful!" I cry. "I'll be right there!"

Why am I so excited? I rush down the ladder.

"She'll open the door—quick now."

Pincher is excited too. He laughs. He congratulates me.

"Handy," he cries as soon as we are on the ground, "get the station wagon and bring it into the yard. Park it right here by the infirmary door. And leave the motor running, d'you hear? Do you know the way to the hospital? Good! We'll want to take them in by the emergency exit. Hurry, hurry!"

Handy runs off and Pincher turns to me. "Well? What are you waiting for, Bodkin? Let's get up there!"

We run up the stairs together, he laughing and slapping me on the back. "You're a genius, Bodkin, a genius—ho, ho, ho."

Miss Fein gives me a stern look in the vestibule. What can that mean? Never mind; there isn't time. I give her a wink and click my tongue, but she averts her head, unmistakably in disgust.

I put my mouth close to the iron door. "Miss Rose? I'm here. It's me—Bodkin. May I come in?"

The door opens slowly, and before Miss Rose has a chance to greet me, Pincher throws his shoulder against it and plunges in. He almost knocks her on her back. I take her to me. She puts her hands on my chest and leans her head on them. I put my arm around her and pat her back in a fatherly way.

Pincher gathers the six little boys together. He doesn't bother dressing them; he feels there isn't time, I suppose. But he gets them into their shoes and socks and has them put coats on over their pajamas. Meanwhile, I try to divert Miss Rose. I get her into her coat. She is dressed in her white uniform. Every other minute she glances at me coquettishly and utters a sylphic endearment.

We all crowd together in the vestibule to wait for Handy and the station wagon. Me, Pincher, Miss Rose and the six boys—as well as Miss Fein, who is sitting in the corner and looking at me in a way which is really disconcerting.

"Are you truly taking me away, then, Bodkin?" says Miss Rose.

"Of course, my dearest."

"Ah, how beautiful," she sighs. "It is like a dream . . . to the warm countries, you said—how beautiful—"

"But, Miss Rose, my dear," says Pincher, "you really must try to cooperate a little—"

"Eh?"

"I mean, you must try to remember what it was you gave to these boys—what drug was it you gave them? It will make it much simpler for the doctors to find the proper antidote, my dear, if you can tell us."

"Drug?" she says dreamily. "I gave them no drug."

"Well then? What was it you *did* give them?"

"A sweet, a magical potion," she says, looking up at the walls as though she could see through them to a wonderful faerie land. "It is a lovely drink. Bodkin and I will send you a bottle from the warm countries. There isn't time now, or I would brew some for you this very moment—"

"Ah God," says Pincher in exasperation. "Do you have the formula written down somewhere at least?"

"It is all in here," she says, pointing to her head. "It is very, very complicated . . ."

"But the *anti*dote, Miss Rose!"

"Antidote, Mr. Pincher? But there is no need for an *anti*dote. These little boys, look how happy, how well behaved they are now . . . why do you imagine they need an *anti*dote for anything, Mr. Pincher? Eh?"

Pincher rolls his eyes at me and sighs. "There's no talking to her, Bodkin, no talking—"

"So many beatings, so much abuse, so little love—such wretchedness, such horror . . . what a place this is, Mr. Pincher! What a terrible, terrible place. When the staff is not whipping them, they are whipping themselves. They are not even savages. Savages are at least wild. But these little boys, Mr. Pincher—what are they? Merely abusive. Abused and abusive, yes."

"Well then, Miss Rose, what would you suggest we might do to improve conditions here, eh?" says Pincher, winking askance at me. I think he is enjoying this a bit in a hysterical sort of way.

"Im*prove?*" says Miss Rose. "Why, you have simply got to burn the place down—begin all over . . ."

"Do you hear, Bodkin?" cries Pincher, laughing madly. "Conflagrations! The woman wants conflagrations!"

"Ah," says Miss Rose, looking up and clasping her hands to her breast, "if only I had realized this sooner! I should have been making my potions all along. One dissolves, one disappears, one has wings, one finds a better place . . . how calm I am, how serene, how wonderful everything is—what do I care any more about anything? What do I care about your antidotes, Mr. Pincher? Even if it were fatal, my potion, I wouldn't care. What does it all come to, this life? A stink—indeed, indeed . . . a stink. And if these little boys should die? Well? What of it? The world will not miss them, alas, and at least . . . at least they will have seen a brighter picture before the end—and how bright it is indeed! Even you, Mr. Pincher, are all in lovely colors right now. You are even handsome—come, let me give you a kiss on the mouth, eh?"

"Later, Miss Rose," says Pincher, embarrassed. "You'll kiss me later, my dear."

"But there will be no later. Likely we shall never meet again . . . because I intend never to return."

"Oh, you'll return. Don't worry. This is just going to be a little va*ca*tion, you see. After all, how would we ever get along with*out* you, Miss Rose?" He winks at me.

"You'll get along, you'll get along. I intend to die in bliss in Bodkin's arms, by the sea, in the warm countries, the warm countries . . . but perhaps you would like to join us, Mr. Pincher? Perhaps we might even take these boys with us—eh, Bodkin? What a wonderful idea! Oh, please, please say yes, my love. I will give them potions the day long, I will mix them in fresh pineapple juice . . . lovely, lovely . . . and they will be no bother, no bother at all, I promise you."

"By all means, then," I say, "let's take as many people as you like."

"Ah, you're so sweet, Bodkin, so good-natured . . . but what are we standing here for? Come, my love, let us go . . . you haven't changed your mind, have you?"

I draw her closer to me. "No, no . . . just don't worry—we're waiting for the station wagon. Handy is going to drive us to the airport, you see. We are going by superjet—to Southern California . . . swell beaches there—"

"Ah, Southern California—and by superjet too! How wonderful!"

"Pitiful, pitiful," mutters Pincher, sucking his teeth noisily.

He turns to the six boys, all of whom are slumped on the floor against the wall. "Tell me, boys, what did Miss Rose call that drink she gave you before—hm?"

They only look up at Pincher and smile.

"Can't you hear me!" he cries.

"Potion," says one of the boys.

"Magic," says another.

"They can speak, at least!" says Pincher. "What color was it, hm?"

"Purple," says one.

"No, it was green," says another.

"No, no, blue," says another. "And it have pink stripes . . . and it taste so good . . . mmm—"

"Well, do you all agree at least that it tasted good?"

They nod their heads and mumble. Yes, it tasted good. "Sweet . . . real sweet—"

"Now we're getting someplace," says Pincher. "It was sweet. Now! What *kind* of sweet? Hm?"

"The kind of sweet what make everything look orange. You are ten feet tall, Mr. Pincher. Like a mountain."

"No. He is little. Mr. Pincher real little. Like if I hold out my hand he will walk up it, like a white mouse. Except he is green. And he have a voice like Elvis Presley."

"But it ain't even that kind of sweet at all," says another. "In fact, it is a sweet what is like sour. But like a good sour. Like buttermilk with chocolate cake . . . mmm . . . that make everybody have wee-bitty heads—"

A car horn blows: Handy in the station wagon. Pincher snaps into activity and tries to herd the six boys down the stairs. He implores them, commands them, curses them, but it's no use. They sit in a daze and smile at him like mystics. It's aggravating. We'll have to carry them down, Pincher decides. Meanwhile, Miss Rose looks on calmly, at the edge of ecstasy. Pincher cradles a boy in his arms and takes him down the stairs, and I do likewise. Six boys, three trips; we work fast, me and Pincher—buddies is what we are. Then we go back up and get Miss Rose. We support her by the armpits, and she comes down the stairs with the air of one who is going to her coronation. Majesty is immanent, waiting somewhere out there ahead of her, in the night, waiting to shower divine rights all over her. She is a bride on her way to a groom of infinite promise, some potentate of the spirit; it is not a sly Jew like myself that she has in her mind's eye.

Pincher slips in beside her in the front seat and shuts the

door. "Bodkin!" she wails in terror from within. I can just make out her face through the steam and frost on the glass. The fumes rise out of the exhaust pipe. Her voice is muffled; I am not even quite sure I heard it. The door is sealed. The windshield wipers go clack-a-clack, a seditious music, like the bones of the minstrels.

"Miss Rose," I cry. "Don't be afraid—"

The wagon skids and slides out of the yard, missing the flagpole by inches. Something that sounds like Miss Rose's voice is howling above the engine.

I return to the infirmary to collect my reward. Miss Fein, where are you? Here she is, already straightening the place out, making the beds with her lovely hands—fresh linens for the sick. A pessimistic gesture; how does she know there will be other sick little boys? She looks at me over a pillow she is fluffing, and presses her hand into it. She clutches it to her belly like a shield—from what? She looks at me sternly; where is the intimate, inviting glance of old? Where is the lust in her eyes? The top button of her uniform is undone.

"I heard you before," she says in that Southern drawl—not melodious, not melodious—a gleam of malice in her Jewish eyes. "You called me vulgar and lewd. I don't like that. And I don't like how you went about deceiving that darling old woman. In fact, Mr. Bodkin, I don't like you—hear? Get out."

SOLUTION

The sitting room is as good a place as any, so I go there. I brood. The empty building is even pleasant; everybody is still in the mess hall, sopping up the Technicolor. An hour goes by. Three policemen walk through the courtyard. Pincher is with them, chattering away. He looks at me worriedly as he passes my window, and then they all enter the door that leads to the infirmary.

A few minutes later Pincher returns to tell me all about it. He whispers; he is upset and nervous. Apparently the hospital people found it necessary to report the Miss Rose incident to the police because of the state laws on narcotics.

Further, when the police arrived and questioned Pincher, he told them about Page. They promptly made a few phone calls and discovered that Doberman had not observed the proper formalities in reporting Page's death. They became concerned; "fishy" is the word they used, much to Pincher's dismay. Two of them are up there now making an investigation of the infirmary, and the third is having a talk with Doberman. The policeman discovered him sitting at his desk in complete darkness. "And this *too* must have looked quite 'fishy,' Bodkin. Sitting there with the lights off!" Pincher tells me all this in one breath and then runs back across the yard to the infirmary.

Suddenly the mess hall vomits the madhouse into the night; the boys stream into the courtyard and fill up all of the wings. Everybody is Jack the Ripper tonight; that was the movie they saw. Even the staff look grim and shifty. Shut up in this place with one hundred and eighty Jack the Rippers is not one's idea of an evening. I'm glad there are a few cops around.

Nod passes my sitting room and pokes his head in the door to whisper that he will come down as soon as the Days have gone and everybody is in bed.

At nine o'clock the Days throw the keys at me and disappear. There is quiet everywhere. A light snow is falling.

Nod skulks in on his toes, dressed in overcoat, scarf, galoshes and that hat of his with the furry earflaps. He hands me the little notepad, crumpled and stained, just as Weasel blows in, a heavy draft at his back. Nod doesn't like this and moves quickly to retrieve the paper, but I shift away from him. I have already begun to read. He mutters, looks at Weasel with hostility and retreats to a corner of the room. Weasel senses immediately that something is up; he comes around behind my chair and reads over my shoulder.

In the main it is exactly what I knew it would be. A private, literary effort, full of self-recriminations—complete fantasy, in fact, a futile, rapturous attempt at self-improvement; one can almost hear Doberman saying between the lines, "Lift me up, lift me up." So tidy is it, however, that I have the feeling it was written with a view to future publication. There isn't a grammatical unseemliness in the whole revelation.

In it he recounts, with a creeping, Gothic horror, the events of the night of Page's death—in a prose that is Parnassian and reeking with inversions and other odors; it's quite moving, actually. A certain tension is created between the event as I remember it and the oceanic grandeur of Doberman's rendering. It comes off hilariously. I'm ready to weep. The alleged attempts on his life were staged by himself, as I had suspected. He reveals this immediately in purple intimations. He wanted to attract attention to himself but succeeded only in drawing more pity. This drove him deeper into despair. What he dreamed of was a shake-up. If ever he could get people to look up and listen, he felt he might make a big change in the place—invert the order, just like his prose, and send brutality and disputation cowering off into a corner somewhere. The night of Page's death he parked his car in the woods and attached the bomb to the ignition. But he did it halfheartedly. The specter of futility rose up before him like his own face in a mirror. He was beginning to understand that nobody cared whether he was killed or wasn't killed. He set out across the field toward the rear of the building: "I felt as if a force were drawing me."

A force drawing him; probably he did. A reader has to give of himself and make certain allowances. He climbed up the fire escape to the third-floor bedroom in my quarters. He heard the arguments; they offended his delicate sensibilities. He heard Miss Rose's premonitions; they gave him ideas. Then after a bit he discovered Page.

That, in brief, is the sequence of events he rehearses.

The extravagant meditations, however, are what give this literary effort its peculiar quality. He entertains the notion that he had, in fact, desired just such a death and that he had been thinking at the moment of finding Page's body that just such an "event" was needed to shake the place up. There is a lofty section in which he speculates that maybe he had "willed" Page's death. It makes you want to throw up. He has had a twisty education; reared on the ineffable, he has developed a really unbecoming taste for it.

Not able to restrain his rhetorical inclinations, he goes on to develop himself in the role of killer. The entire institution is a "slaughterhouse for the soul," he says, and therefore he who presides over it is not only a killer, but a mass murderer into the bargain. "I had indeed killed little Page a long time before that fateful night—killed him, dear God, along with all the other children here." Which leads him to the conclusion that the "actual" death of Page was "good" —and during the development of this remarkable opinion, he comes up with an admittedly lively stroke: "It is one thing to excommunicate a heretic from a temple, but quite another to excommunicate an innocent from a desecration." The man could make a name for himself as a moralist, no question about it.

The whole effort is a few thousand words long. It is good in its way; I wish he had gone on for a few more pages. The train of his thought is spectacular and takes one through very dark passages—just the sort of disaster I might enjoy looking over of an evening. But at this moment, what with Weasel reading and grunting over my shoulder, and little Nod peering at us from the far wall, quivering with fear and anger and irreproachable hostilities, I don't get much of a kick out of the prose, well ordered though it is. In fact, my stomach hurts, I have a bad taste in my mouth, I am trembling with nicotine, and my scalp has begun to itch.

Suddenly Weasel snatches the notepad out of my hands. "Where did you get this, boy?" he says, shaking it at Nod.

"From Doberman's drawer."

Greatly excited at this, Weasel announces to me that we have to go right to the police. He takes the prose the same way Nod does. Doberman even underlined the sentence "I killed James Page," and it sticks out like a sore thumb. In print it wouldn't be so bad. It would be in italics, ghostly; one might not even see it. People who design type know that just those words that an author wants to let out at the top of his voice are the ones that ought to be italicized into wisps and murmurs. Anyway, "I killed James Page" is the only sentence that Weasel, like Nod, understands. He doesn't admit to this, but I divine it at once.

I try to reason with him, but there's nothing for it; I might just as well save breath. I have a mind to boot him one, but he is bigger than me, so perhaps patience is the best line to take.

"We got to find Pincher," he decides. "He will know just how to do and what to do. I think he is up in Doberman's office with Doberman and the cops. Come on. We will get him out of there and talk to him first."

He wants both Nod and me to accompany him, but Nod is afraid to leave the quarters because of Blinken. "Those boys up there will kill him, Bodkin. *Some*body got to stay."

"Nobody is killing nobody, boy," says Weasel. "Mr. Ashe is right next door, and he hears every little pin that drop. Mr. Ashe he even hears a pin or two that *don't* drop. So never you worry."

Nod is not convinced and implores me to stay while he accompanies Weasel, but I am not about to let these two fanciful creatures out loose unescorted in the night with such a vibrant bit of literature in hand.

Weasel insists that Nod come along. "You got to tell the police just where you found it, boy. You always screaming about how Doberman kill the Page, ain't you? Well now? Now you got you proof! And now you are going to back down? Hum?"

So the three of us run through the cold yard to the door leading to Doberman's office.

Pincher greets us in the vestibule authoritatively. "Sorry, gentlemen," he says, showing us the palm of his right hand. "No one is allowed upstairs. Mr. Doberman is having a consultation. I have orders to admit absolutely no one—" He looks at Nod. "Why aren't you in bed, son?"

"Listen, Pincher," whispers Weasel, holding up the note-pad. "Doberman killed the Page! That's right—what you making goggle-eyes at me for, man? Look. Proof. A confession . . . right here, see? Handmade by the Doberman himself. Signature and the whole shot."

"Impossible—" gasps Pincher, but he decides he better have a look. He unlocks the rear door to the treasurer's office, and the four of us go in there where we can talk.

Pincher shuts the door, seizes the notepad at once and begins to read. He stares at the paper hard and knits his brows. By the third page, though, he begins to relax, and a condescending little smile breaks out on that big foolish face of his. I am ready to take back everything unkind I have ever said about the man; a decent fellow, is Pincher.

"Why, this is no confession, Mr. Weasel," he laughs when he finishes reading. He slips the notepad in his breast pocket.

"What you mean!"

Pincher lets himself down into the treasurer's swivel chair and puts his feet on the desk. Evidently he is quite at home here. "I *mean*, Mr. Weasel, that this is merely *lit-er-a-ture*. Do you understand me?"

Weasel is nonplused. "You mean he don't mean what he say there, Pincher? Is that what you mean?"

"Exactly."

"Shoot! That is just like what *Bod*kin said too!" Weasel stamps his foot. "Well, I tell you what. You just give it here. I will show it to them *po*lice up there. We will see what *they* got to say."

"'Another stupid nigger'—*that* is what they will say, my dear Weasel."

"Hum?"

"Correct. And is that what you want? You, who are always so concerned about bringing shame and humiliation on our race? Is it?"

Weasel is so confused, so frustrated, that he is close to tears. He respects Pincher, even admires him, and envies him too in a curious way. Weasel tries to carry on the dispute, but his conviction has been shattered. Everything has come down on his head at once: first he is fired, and now this. He can't get his bearings; he is like a man setting out across a deserted street who, by the time he gets to the white line in the middle, suddenly finds himself surrounded by traffic gone haywire—nobody paying attention to signs, cars driving on the sidewalk and the wrong side of the street.

By now Weasel has a lump in his throat that gags him a little when he talks. He cannot even find an object against which to direct his anger. He relents, his arms flapping loosely against his thighs, and mutters to himself. For a moment he reminds me of Boober.

"The essential thing," says Pincher, "is to forget about all of this nonsense at once." With that he goes into the little john beside the safe, leaving the door open, rips off the pages and flushes them down the toilet. "There now, that's the end of it."

Nod, who all the while has remained silent with his mouth open, bursts out, "What did you do? What did you do?" He starts to cry.

"Shh, shh," Pincher admonishes frantically, one finger over his lips. "They'll hear you upstairs, child!"

"Let them hear!" says Nod.

Weasel claps his hand over Nod's mouth and twists the boy's arm behind his back. "You heard Mr. Pincher, didn't you, boy? He said shh. And that mean shh. You must not fret. They is complications here, and you, boy, are not smart enough to understand. But Mr. Pincher, he knows. He has been to college. That paper you found don't mean what it say. Understand?"

Nod struggles for breath and his tears run over Weasel's knuckles, but he quiets down after a bit.

The boy has been witness in his short life to too many

unpunished, unrevenged, obscure crimes which for one reason or another he cannot speak of. He clams up as soon as we are alone together in the yard. There is no telling what is on his mind.

I don't press him. I take him upstairs to his quarters, and immediately he walks across the bedroom to put his hand under Blinken's nose to feel his breath. Then, satisfied that his friend is alive, he looks up at the ceiling and listens. I stand beside him quietly for a minute or so. He slips into his own bed without removing even his shoes or hat, and lies on his back with his hands cupped behind his head.

"Why don't you get into your pajamas, son?" I say. "You'll be much more comfortable."

He makes no answer. I'll let him have his way. I start to leave, but pause at the door. "Are you okay, Nod?"

He still doesn't answer. I go on down to my sitting room and stare out the window at the falling snow. As I watch, Weasel comes out of the treasurer's office and walks solemnly across the yard to his quarters.

An hour passes, then the three policemen appear in the yard. Likely they have finished with Doberman and are on their way out. Suddenly Boober, Trembley and Ashe converge on them and begin to assail them with questions. Now Pincher hurries out to his car, waving good-by obsequiously to the cops, and drives off.

There are footsteps on the second floor—somebody in shoes. I ascend the stairs and discover Nod just leaving his friend's bedside. He glances at me, returns to his own lower bunk and sits on the edge of it.

"Better wait on that business, you two, until morning," I say. "Go on and lie down, Nod. Try and get some sleep."

He shivers and convulses. His head jerks downward. His

hands grip the bottom of his thighs, and his knees spread apart as he vomits on the floor. I go over to him and put one hand on his shoulder until he's had it out.

At last he lifts his head and stares fixedly at something on the other side of the room, though there is nothing there. He wipes his mouth with his forearm and looks up at me.

I walk at once to Blinken's bed and remove the blankets. Page's corpse, I remember, looked not very different from a boy asleep—almost like Blinken does now. Except that Blinken is breathing soundly, though for a moment I thought that perhaps he wouldn't be, soundly or otherwise. The horror in Nod's face is infectious. Now he is standing up.

"What's the matter, son?" I say.

"They done it," he says hoarsely. "Like they said they would. They kill my friend."

I try to make my voice as comforting and gentle as I can. I reassure him that his friend is alive, but he pays no attention.

"They poison him," he says. "He is stiff. All the life is gone out of him."

"No, no, son. Look, see for yourself. He's alive."

I remove the blankets once again, and slipping a hand under Blinken's shoulders, lift him up gently. "Come on, son, wake up for a minute. We want to talk to you."

"Hmm?" He rubs his eyes sleepily and then glances bewildered from me to Nod.

"See, Nod?" I say. "Your friend's okay . . . Right, Blinken? Aren't you okay?"

"Huh?"

Nod steps backward and puts both hands to his temples. "No, no," he says. "You are dead—lay down. Let him lay down."

What should I do? I don't know what to do. Nod is edging slowly toward the door. I ease Blinken down and pull the blanket over his shoulders. He is asleep at once, was never properly awake.

Nod has moved out into the hall. He looks at me through the doorway, but I can't make out his face because the light is behind him. Then he takes a step and looks up the staircase, and the light catches his face; he is biting his upper lip with his lower teeth.

The voices in the yard rise briefly and my stomach turns. Nod is out of sight, running up the stairs, and I hurry into the hall. He is nearly at the top of the staircase. He has a knife—a dull, sorry butter knife from the mess hall—in his hand. I run up after him, and when I reach him in the middle of the third-floor bedroom I take the wrist of his knife hand and twist it up behind his back. Just before I put my hand over his mouth he manages to cry out, "They killed my friend," which doesn't disturb even one of the light sleepers. On our way out, Punzel shifts uneasily in his bed, but he doesn't awake.

The only thing to do is to keep Nod with me for the night in my sitting room. I take him down the stairs slowly; he struggles, so I have to keep his right arm behind his back and my hand over his mouth. He wiggles around, but I have had experience, and also once read a Victorian translation of a Japanese booklet on the various arts of self-defense. He repeatedly tries to force his mouth open so that he can take a bite out of my palm. When we reach the second landing he kicks my shin with the heel of his left foot and stamps on my toe. This is clever of him, and only goes to prove, once again, that a man may retain his cunning after his reason has departed. In pain and surprised, I loosen my hold just long enough to let him slip away. He runs down the stairs like an animal in terror and bursts out the door into the courtyard. By the time I reach the door, he has already engaged the attention of the three policemen. Boober, Trembley and Ashe are still in a huddle with them.

I will have to venture out into the cold night then, and settle everybody down. First I get my coat from my sitting room though, and take my time with the buttons; I will have to be calm, serene. I will have to show these men of the law that I am a person who knows whereof he speaks, a person for whom a disturbed child at midnight with a butter knife in his hand is a matter of course.

The sergeant is a man in middle age. His name is Gold. His hat is tucked under his arm. He is bald on top, with a fringe of closely cropped black hair. His nose is hooked, a fleshy mole on the end. His eyes are tiny and dark and twinkle. His lips are extremely thin, and good-natured somehow. He has a very heavy shadow of a beard, and his cheekbones, though not especially exotic or large, are protuberant. He has a deep cleft in his chin. His face is long and narrow. He doesn't eat properly, I'd say. His breath is rank—bad stomach. Already I feel as if we are old friends.

He is troubled by Nod's remonstrances. I think that he must be a very broad mind because he gives the boy a hearing. I suspect that he also wants to impress the other two policemen, who are undoubtedly rookies. They affect the attitude of bored, cynical veterans, but they are so young and radiant with inexperience that I am embarrassed by them.

One of them is assigned to watch my quarters, while the other tags along beside Sergeant Gold, who escorts Nod and me up to Doberman's office. Boober, Trembly and Ashe are left behind, and are clearly offended at being shut out of it. But they will have more fun speculating in the dark. The rookie assigned to my quarters is instructed to check "each and every bed." Apparently the good sergeant is not entirely unmoved by the passion of Nod's convictions. He assures me, however, that he doesn't believe a word of it, and that his desire to question Doberman and myself about the boy's "fantasies" is a mere formality, "just for the record."

To Doberman he says the same thing. A tactful man, the sergeant. Nevertheless he is tense, and he can't disguise the fact that he is troubled and suspicious.

It is clear from the first exchanges between Doberman and the sergeant that just as Pincher said, the authorities have suddenly taken a disproportionate interest in our madhouse because of the magic potion, and the death of Page—upon which are attendant certain formalities Doberman failed to observe. Apparently, however, the sergeant had departed earlier on friendly terms, with most of the difficulties resolved, and his unexpected return worries Doberman—whom we have caught at an unfortunate moment anyway. He has fallen into one of his heavy moods, from which he is not able to extricate himself easily. This isn't good. The sergeant needs reassurances. A jolly Doberman would have been much better.

Nod falls silent on entering the office. He is nervous and breathing heavily and stands very close to the sergeant.

The young rookie sits in a corner of the room, a clipboard on his lap, and with great seriousness proceeds to write as soon as the sergeant announces that the formal interview has begun. "Just a few questions," he tells us. There are, in fact, only two questions addressed to Doberman: "Did you kill James Page?" and "Did you ever commit to writing any statement which might be construed in any way to be a confession to the murder of James Page?" To both questions Doberman answers no.

Nod stamps his foot, and his eyes fill with tears again. "What do you ask *him* for, man?" he cries to Sergeant Gold. "The Doberman he is a *kill*er. He don't tell you nothing but lies. You got to ask *Bod*kin, see? Because he *seen* that paper what Pincher flushed down the john."

"Settle down, son," says the sergeant. "I'm getting to Mr. Bodkin."

"But I mean you got to ask Bodkin about the paper, see? Then you will know I am not crazy like they say, see? That monkey Pincher, he flushed it down the john . . . I could kill his ass—"

"Easy now."

"I mean, just ask him. Ask Bodkin. Just about the paper at least. Don't ask him about no murder. He can't see a dead man. He can't even see Blinken is dead, see? His body stiff and the life gone out of him . . . and Bodkin say, 'No, he is alive.' Alive! No, just ask about the paper. Because that's all he knows about is paper. Just ask him this: 'Was there a handmade confession by the Doberman himself?' And 'Did that monkey Pincher flush it down the john?' That's all, see?"

"Listen—" begins the sergeant.

"Listen nothing! Mr. Bodkin, he knows. He know exactly what I know. Go ahead, man, ask the Bodkin. What you afraid of? *I* know. You afraid, see, that then you will have two peoples what know the same terrible thing. And then that mean you are going to have to *think,* man. And that hurt your brain, I know."

The sergeant pulls the boy's earlobe as though it were the string on a little bell. "Quiet, son."

Nod smiles up at him. "Oh no, now that ain't hard enough. You got to pull harder than that if ever you expect to hurt *this* boy. Bodkin, go on and tell him about the paper ... please, up and *tell* him—"

I smile at him reassuringly. Nod smiles back and wipes a tear from his cheek with the back of his hand. He then winks triumphantly at the rookie who is playing stenographer in the corner.

"All right, Bodkin," says the sergeant. "Did you ever see any piece of writing with Mr. Doberman's signature on it which might be construed as a confession to the murder of James Page?"

"No ... no, I didn't," I say.

We are silent for a minute. The sergeant has his left arm folded across his chest, the forefinger of his right hand under his nose, and he is looking at the floor as though something very important but elusive were lying there.

Nod says, "What d'you mean 'No,' Bodkin?"

"You're just seeing things, Nod," I say. "Take it easy. That's not what that paper said at all."

"What do you mean *see*ing things? *Sure* I am seeing things. I am seeing 'I killed James Page' in Doberman's handmade writing, and you seen it too. How come you lie, Body? What are you trying to do? Up and *tell* him, Jew! Tell the *po*lice about that paper!"

"Listen, Sergeant," I say, "I'd better take the boy back to his quarters. This kind of thing isn't really healthy for him. He's working himself into a fit."

"How come you talk to that cop like I'm not in the room no more?" says Nod.

"Go ahead, Mr. Bodkin," says the sergeant in an undertone. "That's about all I wanted to ask you, anyway."

"How come you talk like I'm not in the *room!*" says Nod. He clenches his fists.

"Easy, son," says Doberman.

"And don't *you* 'son' me neither."

"Let's go, Nod," I say.

"Get back. Don't touch me. I say, don't come *near* me." I continue to advance toward him slowly. "Just take it easy."

"Hold it," he says. "Wait . . . don't come near me now. I warn you, Jew. One more step and you will be sorry." He picks up a wooden chair and sets his shoulders and feet like a boxer.

"Don't start in now, Nod. Put it down." I stop a few feet away.

"That's right," he says. "Just stay right there. One more step and I will throw it through the window, I promise you."

"And what good do you suppose that will do you, son?"

"What good? It will make a big hole in the window, that is what good. Ha, ha—"

"Easy, son."

"Don't 'son' me, I told you before. Don't 'son' me, don't 'son' me!"

"Put that chair down, boy," says the sergeant firmly. This is not wise.

"Who are you talking to? I'm no *boy*. You baldheaded mother-fucker, don't you call *me* boy. My brother he will whip your ass he hear you call me that. I am William Nod, and don't you forget it."

The sergeant catches the rookie's attention; he makes a

slight motion of his head and shifts his eyes. The rookie understands immediately; he slowly rises from his chair and starts to edge around the wall in an attempt to get Nod from behind.

Nod catches on to this quickly. "You stay where you are too, baby face."

The rookie blushes and then looks sheepishly at the sergeant. Nod takes a step backward, closer to the window. While his attention is still diverted to the rookie, I manage with a quick movement to kick the chair out of his hands. I grab him by the back of the collar and twist one of his arms up behind his back.

"Let me go!" he cries. "You bastard, you bastard Jew! I hate you, I hate you, let me . . . let me go!"

"Easy now, son. What you need is a little fresh air. Let's go."

"Don't *push* me! I said, don't *push* me!"

"Go easy on him, Bodkin," says Doberman.

This I don't like. In fact, I don't like it at all. I pause and turn around and look at Doberman. He flushes and averts his eyes. Nod is still struggling desperately in my hands. I loosen my hold and let him go. I'm thinking it might not be such a bad idea really to let them all kill each other.

Nod scrambles to a corner of the room and manages to get another chair in his hands. The sergeant gives me a look of displeasure; he supposes that I am an incompetent. The rookie advances toward Nod.

"Don't move, nobody . . . don't nobody move—get back, I said!"

"I'll handle this," says Doberman in an undertone.

The rookie stops.

"Yeah, that's right, you handle it," says Nod.

"Now, son . . ."

"Come on and *han*dle it, I said! Come and kill me like you done Page—come on, come on! What you afraid of? Nobody is going to see it anyway. They all *blind* men, ain't they? They will come up and look at that shiny bullet in my head and say, 'That poor little boy just drop dead. I wonder how come he just drop dead like that.' Right? So what you afraid of, child? Huh? Huh?"

"I am not afraid," says Doberman gently. "I am only worried—worried about you, son. You are the only person in this room right now who is afraid."

Nod laughs. "You call *me* afraid? I will show you how afraid I am."

"You don't have to show me anything, son."

"But I am going to show you anyway, see. I am going to make such a big splash in this window that the fresh air rush in here and give everybody penumonia so quick they will drop dead on the spot. That is how afraid I am."

"I see," says Doberman with a melancholy smile. "But what will you do after that? What will you do, son, when everyone is dead, hm?"

"What will I do? I will laugh. Because then, see, my brother is going to rush in *too* through that splash and say, 'Wake up, Dead. I got to kick some ass around here.' "

"Easy now, son."

"And then all you dead, see, you going to rise up, and he is going to put you in a line down there in the snow, and strip you naked as you were born and say, 'Listen here'— that's right—'Listen here!' That is just how he will say. And *then* we going to see who is afraid and who is not afraid."

"Calm down, son."

"Shut up, I said! Shut up, shut up! 'Listen here!' he will

say. 'I know who kill Blinken and the Page, and I don't like it. I don't like how everybody here beat on my little brother Nod and call him crazy *nei*ther. You are all liars and killers and brutalities and lunatics. Gentlemen, I got to do some stuff in this place.' That is just how he will say, you better believe it. So don't let me see you *wor*ry about me no more, Mr. Doberman. I don't need it, your worry. I shake this chair in your face, and I worry about *you*."

"Bodkin . . ." Doberman looks at me, sadly, for assistance.

"But my *bro*ther now, he don't worry, no. He laugh like a thousand alligators, you bet. His gloves go *rata-tata-tat* . . . solid gold, yes, like a flash in the cloud. Like a light and a thunder. Oh, is he going to beat some people up? You bet. One, two, three, four, five, everybody. And they is going to be blood in this happy-house everywhere, and then it will be not so happy no more. It will be an *un*happy-house, with everybody naked and beat up and wailing in their blood . . . and then you know what he is going to do? He is going to get him a shovel and a *trom*bone, and he will bury you live with the one and play *sad* songs till you dead again with the other. And then? Ha, ha! Me and him will be so lonely, I tell you, that we won't know what to do with ourself but laugh. Oop. Stay back. Watch this chair—one, two . . . look out—"

ABOUT THE AUTHOR

Barton Midwood was born in Brooklyn in 1938. In 1959 he graduated from the University of Miami, and now once again lives in Brooklyn with his wife and two children. His stories have appeared in the *Paris Review, Esquire* and the *Transatlantic Review*. *Bodkin* is his first novel.